P.

A Chocolate Centered Cozy Mystery Series

Cindy Bell

Copyright © 2016 Cindy Bell

All rights reserved.

ISBN-13: 978-1726478304

ISBN-10: 1726478300

Table of Contents

Chapter One

The dough against Ally's fingertips relaxed every muscle in her body. By the time the dough was rolled and she had started pressing it into the tart pans, Ally's mind shifted into a peaceful place, guided by her grandmother's subtle humming. That soft repetitive sound was one of the most treasured memories of her childhood. It still brought her a level of comfort that nothing else could. Flour dusted the counter and the sweet scent of the chocolate mixture that would fill the shells wafted through the air. It was a delicious experience for every one of her senses.

"Ready for the oven." Charlotte lifted a tray and slid it inside the oven.

"This one is, too." Ally pressed the dough into the last tart pan then carried the tray over to the oven as well. Once the tarts were in Ally and Charlotte high-fived.

"These are going to be delicious, the pastry looks perfect." Ally smiled. "I wish we made them more often."

"We really should. I'm glad the excuse to do this came up. The cocktail party tonight should be fun."

"Do you think so?" Ally scrunched up her nose. "I'm not so sure about that."

"Why not?"

"I don't know, a room full of politicians, I'm not sure that could be considered fun."

"Some of those people aren't so bad. It's good to make connections with Mayor Malcolm and his associates. I live on the border of Freely now and we have a lot of customers from there so if we ever have a problem it can be beneficial to have a good relationship with those in a position of authority."

"Are you talking about corruption, Mee-Maw?"

"No sweetie, I'm talking about hands washing hands, and what someone in power remembering your name can do for you. The only thing we will ever bribe with, is chocolate." Charlotte laughed. "I wish I could say that the politicians of Freely are all honest, but that wouldn't be honest of me."

"It makes me uneasy to think of schmoozing for the sake of favor."

"It's not for favor, it's just for courtesy. It doesn't hurt to have someone on your side in the event of a disaster. Let's not pretend that you don't use a bit of favor when you need Luke's help."

Ally grimaced and laughed. "Okay you got me there. I see what you're saying."

"So tonight we'll go, we'll serve our luscious chocolate tarts, we'll dance, and hopefully if we ever have a parking ticket in Freely that we can't pay, someone will remember our names."

"Okay, I suppose I'll find a way to enjoy myself then."

"I know one way it would be a lot more fun. Couldn't you get Luke to play hooky?" Charlotte asked.

"Luke?" Ally laughed. "The only time he ever bends the rules is if I'm in trouble. I don't think a stuffy party at a country club counts. Besides, he's excited about this training, it will give him a foot up towards getting a promotion."

"Ah well, I guess a week without him will have to be tolerable then."

"Ten days actually, and it's not," Ally sighed, "at all. I hate to admit it, but I miss him."

"You shouldn't hate to admit it, Ally. It's a good thing to miss someone."

"Is it?" Ally tilted her head from side to side. "Sometimes I'm worried that I'm getting a bit too attached."

"You mean that you're head over heels in love?"

"Stop." Ally sighed and picked up a stray chocolate from the counter. "I've vowed to be as disconnected from him as possible while he's away. He needs to focus, and I need to remind myself that I'm not dependent on him, though I may very much enjoy his company."

"I guess that makes sense." Charlotte scrunched up her nose. "Love was much simpler when I was young."

"And now?" Ally quirked an eyebrow. "What happened to that man at Freely Lakes you were seeing? I didn't even get to meet him."

"Well, it turns out we don't see eye to eye on a lot of things, and to be honest, I am far too old to argue with anyone other than you." She winked. "I don't know, Ally. Sometimes I think it would be nice to connect with someone again, but perhaps I've fallen in love with being single. It's nice not to have any expectations, not to have to worry about someone else's feelings, or cater my decisions to their whims."

"I can agree with that. There's pluses and minuses to both I suppose."

"True. But I can tell you this much, Ally, I might be content on my own right now, but if love presented itself to me, the real kind, I wouldn't hesitate to jump on it. Missing out on something magical only leads to regret." She met her eyes.

"Okay, okay, message received." Ally grinned. "At least we'll both be single tonight. I'll pick you up at six?"

"Perfect. I left you a list on the front counter of things that you should bring to the dinner tonight."

"You should stay with me tonight after the party. The shop is closed tomorrow, we only have some baking to do. We can have a sleepover." Ally leaned close. "I rented that new movie you wanted to see and I've got plenty of popcorn."

"Oh, the one with all of the dancing?" Charlotte wiggled her eyebrows.

"That's the one." Ally grinned. "What do you say?"

"I say, a sleepover is long overdue, and I'd love to."

"Great. I'll make sure that we have plenty of snacks."

"See you tonight." Charlotte kissed her cheek then left through the back door of the chocolate shop. Ally glanced at her phone. No texts, no calls. She took a deep breath and reminded herself that Luke was occupied. Maybe her grandmother was right, being single seemed a whole lot less complicated.

***

When Ally arrived at the cottage a very hungry pot-bellied pig greeted her at the door with a loud snort.

"Oh dear, you are hungry, little piggie." Ally frowned and shuffled him away from the door. "Sorry I'm a bit late, I got caught up with baking." She walked over to the cabinet and pulled out his food. The moment she filled his bowl, Peaches pranced her way into the kitchen. She sat down in front of Ally's feet and meowed repetitively.

"Oh, you think just because I'm feeding Arnold, I have to feed you too, hm?" She put some food in Peaches' bowl and gave the cat a scratch behind the ear. "I missed you today, my friend."

Ally stretched her arms above her head. It had already been a long day, and she had a long evening ahead of her. What she really wanted was a nap, but there was no way of getting out of the party. She had already committed to it. Just as she settled down on the edge of the couch to gather her thoughts, her cell phone rang. She answered it right away.

"Hey Luke. How's the training?"

"It's pretty brutal." He yawned. "How are things in your neck of the woods?"

"Pretty quiet. Oh you know, except for the cocktail party I have to go to tonight."

"You have a date?"

"Nope. Not unless you count Mee-Maw."

"I wish I could be there to go with you."

"Don't worry about that. I'm going to be working most of the night anyway, I'm sure you would have just been a distraction."

"I'm sure I would have been, too. In fact, I try my hardest to make sure that I am."

"Oh trust me, you are usually very successful at that." Ally laughed.

"I'm glad that you think so. I wasn't sure if you even noticed my efforts."

"Oh, I noticed all right. I think when you get back we need to have a long conversation about your distracting behavior."

"Okay. But I can't promise not to distract you."

"I'm counting on it."

Luke laughed. "I'm glad things are okay. The training is interesting, I have to admit, but I had no idea it was going to be this physical, I might be a few pounds lighter by the time I get back."

"Hm, maybe I need to try that training out."

"Absolutely not. You're perfect, just the way you are."

"Aw, that's sweet."

"I mean it. And, I do wish that I could be there."

"Me too, Luke. Have a good night."

"I'm going straight to bed." He yawned again.

Ally hung up the phone and headed for her room to dress. After choosing a simple multi-colored dress that fitted loosely, she tugged a brush through her hair and applied a sparse amount of make-up. Her main intention was not to be noticed. If she could pull that off, it would be a successful night.

The gleam of a barrette that her grandmother had given her drew her attention. She hadn't worn it yet and it would go perfect with the dress. Maybe a little bit of sparkle wouldn't be so bad. She slipped the barrette into her thick, brown hair and looked in the mirror. The silver surface caught the bathroom light and sparkled a little. Satisfied, Ally left the bathroom and gathered her purse. In her mind she ran through the list of things she needed to remember. Pick up the tarts, pick up extra menus, pick up raspberries, pick up Mee-Maw.

"I'd better not forget her." She laughed and

reached down to stroke Peaches' back. She paused in the kitchen and added a bit more food to Arnold's bowl, just in case the evening went late. Then she headed out the door. Freely was a town full of people that she knew from a distance. She remembered faces, and names, from when she grew up in the small, neighboring town of Blue River, but some people had very little idea of who she was as an adult. An event like the cocktail party, was an opportunity to reconnect with people who she had fallen out of touch with. However, she wasn't sure that she could bring herself to be very social. Despite the fact that she took off on her own to college at eighteen, she hadn't overcome a sense of shyness that prevented her from being the life of the party.

Ally parked outside Charlotte's Chocolate Heaven. The wide front window was filled with an assortment of chocolates as well as chocolate cakes, tarts and muffins. Happiness filled Ally's heart as she walked up to the door. Never did she predict that her life would take this turn, but there she was back home, and running the chocolate shop for her grandmother. Inside she gathered the things she needed under the watchful eyes of an assortment of statues and carvings created by local artists. On her way back out the door she double-checked the lock and mentally checked off things on her list.

Once Ally was back in the car she only had one more thing to pick up, her grandmother. Leaves scattered across the sweeping drive that led into Freely Lakes. She continued to drive towards the main apartment building where her grandmother lived. It was under protest that Ally had agreed to the transition, and she still missed having Charlotte living with her. She believed her grandmother wanted her to have the space so that she could explore her own life with a bit more freedom. But it was hard for Ally to think of her grandmother as a woman, who had her own life to explore. That doubt was wiped out the moment that her grandmother stepped out of the apartment. Ally's words caught in her throat at the sight of the figure-hugging dress that her grandmother wore.

"Mee-Maw, you look amazing," Ally said as Charlotte opened the car door.

Charlotte laughed as she settled in the passenger seat. "I'm sure you say that to all the gals you pick up."

"I mean it, you are stunning in that dress."

"Well, thank you. I know it may be a bit much, but it is supposed to be quite formal. I had a lot of fun shopping for this little number." She eyed the colorful frock Ally wore. "That's a nice dress, too."

"Thanks, I wanted to make sure that I wouldn't get too hot."

"Did you remember the tarts? The extra menus? The raspberries?"

"Yes." Ally laughed. "I remembered all of it. I even gave Arnold a little extra food. We're good to go."

"Great. I don't want to worry about anything tonight, other than our tarts being a big hit."

"I don't think we're going to have to worry about that. People love everything we make."

"Most people. But people in high positions can sometimes be more critical because they have access to so much."

"I'm sure the tarts will go over well. I can't wait to eat one myself."

"None of that!" Charlotte laughed. "We have to make sure that as many people as possible get to taste one tonight. And have more than one if they desire."

"I'm a person." Ally frowned and then winked at her grandmother.

"I promise that if they're all gone we'll spend some time tomorrow making more, just for us. I have a chocolate, peanut butter tart I want to try out."

"Okay, good deal." Ally grinned and turned down the long driveway that led to the country club. It wasn't often that they attended events at the country club, though on occasion they had catered there for dessert. Now that Ally saw the parade of expensive cars and well-dressed people that gathered at the semicircle entrance she swallowed hard. Was she underdressed? Her grandmother's outfit seemed to fit in better than the sundress she wore.

"Ready for this?" Charlotte reached over and patted the back of her hand.

"As ready as I can be." Ally nodded.

"You head in first, I'll meet you there. I just want to freshen up in the bathroom."

"Okay."

Chapter Two

Ally carried the tarts through the doors into the main room of the country club. The interior was packed with colorful decorations, an assortment of tables, and was back to back with influential residents of Freely and the surrounding areas.

Ally was greeted by the head of catering, Elisa, who showed her over to one of the catering tables. When Ally set the tray of small tarts down on one of the tables she noticed that there were several other trays of savory finger food lined up beside it. The food smelled amazing. At the very least she would leave with a full belly. While she prepared the table she noticed her grandmother enter the room. She waved and smiled to several people. Her connections ran much deeper in the community than Ally's did. As she liked to mention as often as possible she had once babysat many of the people in town. Ally waved her over to the table.

"Oh, this is a nice spot." Charlotte smiled. "Lots of people will notice us here."

"If they don't, the smell will draw them. I can't wait to dig in."

"The food and drinks will be available before the speeches. I guess the mayor wants everyone to be liquored up before he breaks the bad news about the state of the budget."

"Maybe it will be better news than you think." Ally shrugged. "From what I've heard about him he seems like a smart man."

"He is quite smart. Smart enough to end up with the position of mayor." Her voice grew strained. "Though it was quite a scandal when he was elected."

"Really? Why?"

"He has a bit of a mafia mentality. Not that he's part of the mafia, I'm not saying that. He just has that type of brusque, authoritative nature. Not too many people that work under him take kindly to it."

"I wouldn't either." Ally narrowed her eyes. "That's such an out of date way to handle politics."

"I personally haven't had any problems with him, but if the rumors are true, he's not the kind of man you want to cross. Do you need any help here?"

"No, I can handle it. Why don't you go mingle? You look too beautiful to hide behind a table."

"You are too kind." Charlotte grinned, but didn't hesitate to join a group of women a few feet away.

Charlotte mastered the skill of socializing, while Ally straightened the tablecloth. She put on gloves and then she set out the tarts carefully on some platters on the table. She decorated each one with a few raspberries. The raspberries cut through the richness of the tarts. Although the tarts were fine straight from the fridge, having them at room temperature, so the filling melted slightly, transformed them to something beyond just tasty. The way they were displayed made them look even more attractive. A rush of pride coursed through her as she looked at the tarts. It wasn't so much pride in the product, as it was pride in the fact that she and her grandmother had created them together.

There was little that Ally valued more than being able to spend an entire afternoon baking with her grandmother. She looked across the room to find her. She looked beautiful in the scarlet dress that stopped just above her ankle. Once more Ally marveled at how good her genes were. If at her grandmother's age she looked half as good she would be ecstatic. A waitress came and picked up a tray of tarts to walk around with to serve to the guests.

"Could I try one of those?" A man with dark eyes and a long goatee paused in front of the tarts. She noticed that he had a large camera hanging around his neck.

"Sure, here's a plate." Ally handed him a small plate and a fork to go along with the tart. Then she served one to him.

"Thanks. Wait." He frowned as he looked at the tart. "Is this chocolate?"

"Oh yes, they all are."

"Never mind." He sighed and put down the plate. As he walked away Ally wondered how a man as thin as him could be worried about his waistline. Maybe he had another reason why he didn't want to eat the tart. Her attention shifted to the woman who walked up to her.

"I'll take two."

"Great." Ally smiled and served the woman two tarts. When she looked for her grandmother again she noticed that she'd stopped at a table near the front of the room, at the main table where Deputy Mayor Julia Turnamas sat. They seemed to be having a lively chat. Ally's attention remained on them until she was struck by a flying napkin. Startled, she looked up to see a camera pointed directly at her. She raised a hand to shield her face. Laughter emerged from behind the camera. She caught a glimpse of a goatee. "Weirdo." She narrowed her eyes.

If the photographer heard her, he didn't say a word about it. Ally shook her head and returned her attention to her grandmother. She was easily moving between people having conversations with them. By the time Charlotte made her way back to Ally she looked a bit winded.

"Did you have fun making your rounds?" Ally smiled.

"You know how it is, if we get noticed we get more business. Plus, I just enjoy seeing everyone. Especially tonight, with everyone so dressed up."

"Yes, it's a nice affair," Ally said as a man approached them smiling from ear to ear.

"Your tarts are so delicious."

"Thank you, Mr. Housers." Charlotte smiled. "Would you like another one?"

"I shouldn't." He laughed. "But I will." Ally handed him a plate with a tart on it. "Thank you," he said as he turned and walked back towards his table.

"Looks like another happy customer," Ally

said.

"Yes, it seems like the tarts are a huge hit with the politicians." Charlotte smiled. "If you're under control, I'm going to mingle a bit more."

"I'm fine. Enjoy yourself."

As Charlotte walked off Ally scanned the room again for familiar faces. A lot of the people that she saw were familiar from her childhood, but there were none that she could claim as a current friend. Once more she wished that Luke was there with her. It would have been more fun to observe the party with him at her side. They shared a similar sense of humor that would have made the event more enjoyable. It's good for the shop, Ally reminded herself.

It was hard for her to see the politically powerful gathered together under one roof knowing that the event must have cost quite a bit. She found it hard to believe that it was a necessary cost. Maybe in the long run it made a difference, but to Ally it seemed that the only pockets being lined at this event were those of the politicians.

She pulled out her phone to see if she'd missed any texts or calls from Luke. When she saw there was nothing listed, she sighed and pushed her phone back into her purse.

"Bored?" A man paused in front of the table. He looked to be in his forties, with a mixture of red and brown hair that was reflected both on the top of his head and on his upper lip. She didn't recognize him, but the wry smirk on his lips made her think he shared her views.

"A little." She smiled. "But don't tell anyone."

"Oh, trust me, I won't. I'm not even sure why I'm here." He looked over at the tables closest to the stage. "Those people will never understand what it's like to work for a living."

"It certainly isn't blue collar work." Ally nodded and did her best to signal an end to the conversation by turning her attention to the tarts. However, the man didn't seem to have any interest in letting things go.

"Oh please, would you look at those two?" He rolled his eyes and took another long swallow of his wine. Ally followed the direction of his gaze. She saw Julia and her husband with their hands intertwined and their heads tilted towards one another.

"I think it's sweet."

"Sure, they look like they're in love don't they?" He rolled his eyes again and finished his glass of wine. "But it's all for show. It makes me sick."

"What do you mean it's all for show?" Ally bit into her bottom lip. She didn't usually engage in gossip, but the man seemed as if he needed someone to talk to.

"I mean, he's dying for a divorce, and she refuses to allow it because it will hurt her career. Is that love? Not in my book." He narrowed his eyes and continued to stare at them.

"Maybe they've made up." Ally tilted her head to the side. From everything she saw, there was no hint that the couple was unhappy. If it was an act then it was a very good one.

"No, trust me, they haven't. Everyone around town knows. They are barely married at this point. He would do anything to shake her off him, but she refuses to allow it until her term is up. Probably because she's hoping to get elected as mayor. Trust me, the conservatives in this town are not going to elect a woman that goes through a messy divorce. Nothing bugs them more than the thought of alimony." He chuckled as he pointed at a tart. "This looks good."

"They're very good. Please enjoy one," Ally said as she placed a tart on a plate and handed it to him. She leaned against the table as she watched him have a forkful. "So, what do you think they're actually saying to each other?"

"Here, let me tell you." He peered at them for a moment, then began to mimic their conversation. "Would you please not embarrass me tonight, Kirk? You've already had too many glasses of wine." He paused, then deepened his voice. "Why shouldn't I drink? I should be drunk all the time to put up with you."

Ally tried not to smile, but she couldn't resist. She took on the role of the deputy mayor. "Oh yes, your life is so hard, with all of the money my job provides you."

"I have my own money I don't need yours. You're the one that needs me so that we can look like the perfect couple to the voters in this town."

"Wow, you're really good." Ally laughed a little. "Do you come to these types of things just for the entertainment?"

"I'll admit, I'm a little drunk, but I don't consider these things to be entertaining. It bothers me to see a bunch of fat cats making plans for people who have no say in what happens next."

"How do you know about their marriage?" Ally raised an eyebrow.

"Everyone does." He stared at the couple once more.

Ally studied him. She suspected he might have his own romantic interest in Julia. She decided it was time to stop digging before she found out more than she wanted to know.

"Well, I guess that's how politics works."

"For now." He nodded. Then he shifted his gaze to Ally. "But wouldn't it be great if something happened, to shake them all up a little? To give them a dose of reality?"

Ally looked back at him with concern. "Are you okay?"

"Sure, I'm fine." He chuckled and waved his hand. "Please, ignore the insane ramblings of a bitter man." He straightened up. "I'd better get back to my wife before she thinks I'm getting too chatty."

"Good idea." Ally smiled. "Would you like to take her a chocolate tart?"

"Yes please." Ally placed a tart on his plate.

As he turned away to walk back towards his table a woman with shoulder length, black, curly hair walked over to him. She smiled sweetly at him.

"I was just coming back," he said.

"I thought you got lost." She laughed lightly as she hooked her arm through his. Ally presumed she was his wife.

"Let's go sit down." He handed her the plate.

"These look delicious." She smiled.

"Thanks for the tarts," he said as he looked over his shoulder at Ally.

"Let's go. We don't want to miss the speeches and champagne. We might as well see if these traitors have anything important to say." Ally's eyes widened slightly at her words. The ill-feeling towards politicians obviously ran in the family.

Ally watched as they walked towards one of the tables in the back. She wondered whether his wife knew how interested he was in the deputy mayor's relationship.

"Not my business." She focused on the tarts again and tried to put the conversation out of her mind.

As everyone's glass was being filled with champagne ready for the toast, the deputy mayor took to the small stage at the back of the room. Some of the guests gathered in front of the catering tables so they could get a better view of the stage. The deputy mayor walked up to the microphone and smiled.

"Hello and welcome, friends, neighbors, we are all here for the same reason. We want Freely to continue the long tradition of being the greatest little town to live in. Of course there is plenty of good food, and good wine on tap tonight, but as you enjoy yourself please take the time to remember that a town can only be as successful as its government. We want to make sure that Freely stays a wonderful place to live, so please keep those donations flowing." Her voice waned as she began to cough. At first it was a few delicate sounds, but soon it was outright hacking. She covered her mouth and tried to clear her throat. But the coughing continued. She rested her hands on the podium to steady herself. She continued to cough with such intensity that Ally wondered if she might be choking. She must not have been the only one that considered that as Ally saw her husband give her a glass of water. She stepped back from the podium to drink some of the water. She returned to the podium with the glass of water still in her hand.

"Sorry about that." She smiled and took another long sip of the water. Once she set the glass down on the podium she looked back at the audience. "As I was trying to say, we have some amazing events coming up this year that I'm sure you will all be interested in. It is your support that makes all of these wonderful activities possible in our community..." She started coughing again. "I'm sorry." She looked flustered as she took another sip of water. "I think it's time for the toast." She reached out her hand as someone handed her a glass of champagne. Ally tried to see if she was okay, but from the crowd of people standing in front of her she was out of sight. "If you could raise your glass." She lifted her champagne flute up. "To the future of Freely and its wonderful people." She took a sip of her champagne. She coughed again and took another big sip of champagne then put it next to the water glass on the podium. "Now, if you could please..."

Ally looked up as the deputy mayor trailed off. In the same moment that she looked up, the woman collapsed to the stage behind the podium. A collective gasp rippled through the audience. People lurched forward out of their chairs. Mayor Malcolm rushed forward to her side. When he reached her, he cried out.

"Someone call an ambulance! Right now! She's not breathing."

Ally's stomach churned and her chest tightened at his words.

"What is it? What happened?" Charlotte rushed to her side from the entrance of the room.

"The deputy mayor collapsed. The mayor said she's not breathing. I have no idea what happened." Ally started to move closer to the stage, but she was brushed aside by paramedics that rushed forward. The people in attendance at the party gathered in a tight semicircle near the stage and spoke in hushed voices about what they predicted had happened.

"I'm sure she will be fine, she has to be fine, I was just speaking to her." Charlotte grabbed Ally's hand and gave it a squeeze. Ally offered her a supportive smile, but she wasn't as sure.

"Where were you?"

"I had to duck into the restroom." Charlotte frowned. "This is terrible. I hope she's okay." She clasped her hands together under her chin. The mayor, his face as pale as porcelain, walked up to the podium.

"I'm sorry everyone, we're going to have to end the party early. Please, keep our deputy mayor in your thoughts." The paramedics lifted Julia's body onto a stretcher and prepared to roll her out of the room. Ally tried to look away, but she simply couldn't. The paramedics whisked her out past the crowd and into a waiting ambulance. As they hurried by, Ally could see the woman's glassy stare. It struck her that she was dead. There wasn't hope for her to recover. Charlotte must have seen the same thing because she grabbed tightly onto Ally's hand.

Ally turned towards her grandmother. As she held her hand she wondered what might have happened. Did she have some kind of seizure? Or a stroke? People began to file out through the doors. The decorated tables were abandoned. Some of the delicious food lingered untouched. The staff of the country club all appeared dazed and unsure what to do. Ally could sympathize. Moments before she'd been inwardly criticizing local politicians, and now, one was dead. She turned to look at Charlotte and took a deep breath.

"We'd better clean up."

"Yes, I guess we should." Charlotte shook her head. "I'm going to check with the manager to see if there's anything that I can do to help the staff. This will be a big undertaking for them."

"Okay, I'll get our things organized so that we can stay and help." Ally frowned as she began to pile the tarts into a large white pastry box to take back to the shop. They hadn't planned on having many leftovers. As she began to close the lid, an officer walked up to her. She didn't recognize him, but she didn't know any officers from Freely.

"Ma'am, please leave the box."

"Oh, did you and the other officers want some?"

"Excuse me?" He raised an eyebrow. His bulky frame and stern tone made him more than a little intimidating. She read the name tag on his uniform.

"I'm sorry Officer Frank, I didn't mean to insult you."

"We need you to leave the food because we suspect that there is a chance that the deputy mayor might have been poisoned. All of the food she ingested might have to be tested."

"Oh." Ally stared at him. "Well, we baked these ourselves, there's no chance they could be poisoned."

"There's always a chance." He took the box

from her and carried it with him over to a group of officers. Stunned by the revelation that the deputy mayor might have been poisoned Ally could barely get her thoughts together. As Charlotte walked back towards her, the pinch of her eyebrows indicated something was very wrong.

"Mee-Maw, what is it?"

"We need to leave, Ally, as quickly as possible."

"Okay." Ally didn't take the time to question her further. If her grandmother said leave, they would leave. By the time they reached the car, she needed to know what was going on.

"What is it, Mee-Maw? Can you tell me please?"

"We can expect some visits from the police. The manager told me that the last item she ate was one of the chocolate tarts. The police suspect she was poisoned, and since that was the last thing that she ate, they're focused on it as a possible source right now."

"But that's impossible." Ally shook her head.

"I know it is, you know it is, but neither of us have a badge, do we? Let's just get home before things start getting too wild around here."

"Okay." Ally frowned as she looked back towards the country club. Had she just witnessed a murder?

Chapter Three

On the drive home Ally stared out through the windshield of the car. Her mind replayed the party over and over again. Was there ever a time when she had walked away from the tarts? Did anyone else hover over them close enough to add something to them? She couldn't think of a single moment that she was distracted enough for anything like that to have happened. In fact, the more she thought about it the more certain she was that no one could have done anything to the tarts. Unless they were poisoned after they had left her catering table. It struck her that Charlotte was out of the room when the death occurred. Would that make her look guilty?

"Are you okay?" Charlotte reached over and patted the top of her knee. "You're very quiet."

"I'm fine. It's such a shock. I guess, I'm a little worried about the police suspecting us."

"They don't really suspect us, I mean it isn't

even officially a murder yet. They just have to rule us out. They can test those tarts until their tongues fall off, there isn't a drop of anything but pure ecstasy in them."

"Oh my, you didn't tell them that did you?"

"Huh?"

"You didn't tell them that there was ecstasy in them did you? That's a drug, Mee-Maw."

"Oh no." She laughed. "Don't be silly. I know better than to speak to police officers. If they want to find out any information from me they will have to lock me up."

"Ugh. What a horrible thought."

"Maybe so, but that's the only way I will willingly talk. You see, police often rely on intimidation, and I am not one to be intimidated."

"Maybe not, but aren't you worried at all?"

"No, Ally I'm not. I'm more concerned about who would have done this to Julia. She was a good woman. If someone did this to Julia they are a cruel person. We have to be cautious, a murderer might be on the loose."

Ally parked in front of the cottage and sighed. "I hope the police figure it out fast."

"Hopefully they won't have to investigate anything." Charlotte followed her into the cottage.

"Hopefully." Ally frowned.

"Why don't we just try to enjoy our evening until we find out more?"

"Okay, I'll get the popcorn started. The movie is on top of the DVD player if you want to put it in."

Charlotte turned towards the DVD player. The shrill ring of her cell phone startled her. She took it out of her pocket and answered it.

"And you're sure about this? Well of course, we're happy to cooperate in any way possible. Certainly." She hung up the phone. Ally shifted her attention from the sharp pops of the popcorn in the microwave to look at her grandmother.

"Who was that?"

"Officer John Frank. He called to let me know

it's official." Charlotte tucked her phone into her pocket and closed her eyes for a moment.

"She was really murdered?"

"Yes. It has officially been ruled a homicide. She was poisoned. We can expect a visit from the police for questioning."

"Oh no." Ally cringed. "They think we had something to do with it?"

"They're just doing their job. Right?" She smiled at her. "We have nothing to worry about."

Ally nodded, but she wasn't convinced. "I just can't believe this happened."

"I know, it's horrible." Charlotte shook her head.

"Yes, it is. Now we have to prove that our tarts weren't tainted with anything. But what if someone got to them? What if they slipped the poison inside one?"

"They were never out of our possession. How could that happen? You didn't leave them alone did you?"

"Not even for a second. Unless." Ally's eyes widened.

"Unless what?"

"Well, the waitresses were walking around with them on trays. I guess someone could have slipped something into them then."

"That's a bit far-fetched don't you think?"

"I guess, but it's possible. Or maybe..." Ally said thoughtfully.

"Maybe what?" Charlotte asked.

"Well, after we made them they were at the shop for some time before I picked them up. What if someone broke in and poisoned them then?"

"Did you notice anything out of place at the shop?"

"No nothing."

"We can drive ourselves crazy over this, but we won't know anything for sure until the tests come back on the tarts. Either they will show signs of being poisoned, or they won't, and we'll just have to go from there."

"I can't do nothing and just wait. I need to do something and find out who poisoned Julia," Ally said.

"I agree. We need to get to the bottom of this. I'm sure we can if we work together."

"Are you sure you want to look into the murder? With everyone involved, we could upset the wrong people."

"If they're upset because a murderer needs to be brought to justice, then they aren't people I want to associate with anyway. It can't hurt to have more minds on the case," Charlotte said. "We can figure things out on our own."

"It would be fun to do a little investigating."

"It couldn't do any harm to help the police a bit."

"That's true." Ally nodded. "Where do you think we should start?"

"We should start nowhere now. We should start on this tomorrow, the best place to start is after a good night's rest. We can watch our movie, share our popcorn and try to relax. A stressed mind never finds the truth. We can figure out what really happened if we put our minds to it."

"You're right." Ally emptied the popcorn into a bowl. "Let's get the movie started so we can relax." She carried the bowl into the living room. Arnold followed her every move. Charlotte reached into the bowl and tossed him a few kernels as she sat down beside Ally on the couch.

"Watching movies helps me zone out and clear my head. I think Arnold senses that you're on edge."

"Yes, he does." Ally stroked her hand along his back. "You are one perceptive pig, Arnold." She patted the top of his head.

As they watched the movie, Peaches nestled between them on the couch. Ally tried to enjoy the movie, but she could not get Julia's murder out of her head. As the movie came to an end she stood up and stretched her arms above her head.

"All right, Mee-Maw, I'm going to bed. Let me know if you need anything."

"I'll be fine." Charlotte stood up and gave Ally a tight hug. "I'm sorry our sleepover wasn't exactly ideal."

"It's okay, we'll have the chance for many more."

Charlotte disappeared into her bedroom with Arnold following faithfully behind her. Charlotte's room still had a bed so she could sleep over whenever she wanted to. Ally and Peaches went into Ally's bedroom. Ally lay on the bed. A moment later, Peaches jumped up onto her stomach. She kneaded it a few times, then settled into a ball on top of Ally. Instead of giving her a gentle shove to the floor, Ally stroked her fur.

"What is the world coming to, Peaches? One minute you're giving a speech the next you're dead. The person who did it was probably there at the party with us. How did I miss it? You'd think there would be some kind of sign of what was to come. Instead, Julia never even got to finish her speech." Ally thought about the woman's speech. Was her coughing a sign that she was being poisoned? She struggled to fall asleep as she ran over the events of the evening in her mind.

Chapter Four

When Ally woke the next morning her mind was still on Julia. She tried to recall the woman's every movement. The more she skimmed through her memories for a sign that someone meant Julia harm, the less she trusted them. It was strange how everything could become such a blur all of a sudden.

Though there were many reasons why Ally would have been distracted, it was difficult for her to fathom that a murder had played out right before her very eyes and she hadn't noticed a single thing. Then she recalled the man who sidled up next to her and pointed out the flaws in Julia's relationship with her husband. Was he someone that she should be focused on? He obviously had animosity towards the woman, and her husband. Where had he gone after he left her side? Back to the table with his wife.

The man mentioned that politicians didn't know what it was like to do any real work. Maybe that information would help her get to the bottom of who he was. She decided a good place to start in the investigation was to get a list of everyone who attended the party that night. The only problem with that was access. Would the staff at the country club be willing to tell her that? She picked up her phone and dialed the number of the country club. After three rings a soft, perky voice answered.

"Freely Country Club, this is Belle, how may I help you?"

"Hi Belle, my name is Ally. I'm calling to see if you could do me a favor."

"I doubt it, I'm just the receptionist. Is there a department I can transfer you to?"

"Actually, you're probably the best person to help me. I need to get a copy of the guest list from the party last night."

"Are you some kind of tabloid? I've had enough of your calls already this morning."

"I'm not a tabloid." Ally winced. "I don't work

for one. I live in Blue River, and I was at the party last night. I met an old friend, and we got to chatting. I had every intention of getting her new contact information, but then, what happened with the deputy mayor happened, and everyone left so fast I didn't have the chance to see her again. I can only remember her nickname, but I'm sure if I had a list of names I'd remember who she was. I'd just like the chance to contact her."

"I see." She took a deep breath and sighed. "I'm sorry I didn't mean to be rude. It's just that we've had so many horrible phone calls from people today wanting to know all of the sordid details about the party last night. I just assumed you might be doing the same thing."

Ally grimaced as she realized that she kind of was, but for good reason. She wanted to solve the murder, not publicize it.

"No, I really just want to figure out her name."

"You aren't Ally from the chocolate shop are you?"

"I am," Ally said hesitantly.

"Oh, why didn't you say? Just give me a second." Ally heard the keys tapping on her keyboard. Then she cleared her throat. "I can send it to you if you like. Do you have an e-mail address?"

Ally rattled it off to her. "Thank you for your help."

"No problem. I will send it off to you in just a few minutes. Have a great day, Ally. See you in the chocolate shop soon."

Peaches jumped up on top of her as she hung up. It was a reminder that food was a very important part of Peaches' life. She stumbled to her feet and headed to the kitchen to prepare breakfast for one cat, one pig, and one Mee-Maw. She took her time with the oatmeal and seasoned it just the way her grandmother would for her. By the time Charlotte walked into the kitchen, the aroma filled the air.

"Oh, Ally that smells divine."

"I hope you like it." Ally dished the oatmeal into two bowls for them.

"I could have made breakfast."

"I know that, but once in a while I like to do things for you." Ally kissed her cheek. "You deserve it."

"Thanks darling." Charlotte hugged her. "This is a good way to start the day after what happened last night."

"About that, I was thinking about it this morning. I remember that there was this one man I talked to. He seemed especially bitter towards Julia and her husband. Maybe he had something to do with it?"

"Maybe. I'm sure she had quite a few enemies, as the job she does created them." Charlotte stirred her oatmeal, then took a bite. "Even better than mine!" She smiled.

"Thanks, but it isn't." Ally smiled as she had a spoonful. She checked her e-mail on her phone. As Belle had promised, there was an e-mail with the guest list. "I have a list of people that attended the party. Of course that doesn't include the staff and any plus ones, but it is a start to work from.

I'm going to try to figure out who that man was that I talked to."

"Here let me see, I can probably eliminate a bunch. I'm familiar with just about everyone that was there."

"Oh good, I'll print it off so we can cross out names." Ally sent the list to the printer and then looked across the table at her grandmother. "I know your policy is not to worry, Mee-Maw, but I think it's important we get ahead of this. If there's going to be an investigation, we may even have to shut the shop down during it."

"I understand that. It's not so much that I'm not concerned, Ally, it's that there are things that I can control, and things that I can't. The investigation is something that I can't control. If it leads to the shop being shut down, I can't control that either. What I can control, is whether we try to find out who the killer is."

"I agree." Ally stood up and headed to the printer to retrieve the list of names. When she returned Peaches was perched on the table, about to attempt a bite of her oatmeal.

"Hey!" Ally laughed. "That's mine, you kitty thief."

"Hm, interesting." Mee-Maw rubbed her hands together. "That's something that we hadn't even considered."

"What, that Peaches needs to go to kitty reform school?" Ally shooed her off the table and handed her grandmother the list of names.

"No, that Julia might not have even been the target."

"Why do you think that?"

"Well, we can't know for sure that what was poisoned was intended for her. She could have taken food off her husband's plate. Just like Peaches was about to take a bite of your oatmeal, which considering how good it smells you can't really blame her for, maybe Julia took a bite of something that wasn't meant for her."

"Maybe. I guess we'll know more when they figure out where the poison actually came from."

"If you describe the man to me, I might recognize him."

"He was a burly man, reddish brown hair and a mustache, definitely not a politician."

"No, I can't think of anyone that I know of that looks like that." Charlotte shook her head. "I'll go through the list and eliminate who it definitely isn't."

Charlotte crossed name after name off the list. "These are the only names that I don't know. As for the man you spoke to, he could be one of these people I guess."

"I wonder who he is."

"I do know that Mayor Malcolm invited a lot of local business owners and staff, as well as business owners and staff from other towns that are city service providers."

"He was there with his wife so there should be a plus one."

"Unless she was invited and he was the plus one."

"Good point, Mee-Maw." Ally nodded.

"Those are the ones I don't recognize." Charlotte pushed the list across the table back to Ally. Ally skimmed through the names that remained. There were only a few left.

"I'll see if I can look into them," Ally said as she started looking up the remaining names on the computer.

"I'm going into the shop to get some things organized. Maybe I'll get an idea of what's going on around town while I'm at it."

"That sounds like a good plan."

"I'll catch up with you..."

"Bingo, Scott Brally," Ally said as her grandmother turned to look over Ally's shoulder at the man's picture on the computer screen. "That's the man that was bad-mouthing Julia."

"I don't know him."

"Well, I think I'm going to try to find out as much as I can about him."

"Okay. But just remember if he was that open

54

with you about his feelings, it's not likely that he's the culprit, unless he really wanted to get caught."

"I guess, but something he said really sticks in my mind. He wanted to do something to shake them up, to give them a dose of reality." She tapped the name on the list. "If that was his plan, maybe he doesn't care about getting caught."

"Maybe he was just letting off steam. But see what you can find out, and update me."

"I'll drop you off at the shop and meet you around lunch. Okay?"

"Perfect." Charlotte nodded and had the last spoonful of her oatmeal. "I'll let you know if I come across anything fishy."

Chapter Five

After Ally dropped her grandmother off at the shop she took time to do some searching on her phone. It didn't take long for her to find more information about Scott Brally.

"He owns a garbage business," Ally said to herself as she tapped her phone. "The same business that picks up trash around town. No wonder he thinks politicians have no idea what real work is like." She looked through his information and found that there was an article about him being arrested for assaulting his competitor, but the charges were dropped.

Ally looked through the information to find an address. Once she found it, she plugged it into the navigation application on her phone. When she saw that the drive was over an hour away she hesitated. Did she really want to drive that far just to knock on a man's door? He might not be home, and if he was, he might not answer. She decided to enter the address of his business. It was in close proximity to his home so it was still quite a distance. Instead of driving all that way for nothing she placed a call to his business office, because she believed that there was more of a chance that he would be there. A cheerful voice greeted her.

"Disposal Services, this is Maddie, how can I help you?"

"Hi Maddie. I'm trying to reach the owner of the business, Scott Brally?"

"Oh Scott? He's not in right now. May I take a message?"

"I was wondering if I could schedule an appointment to see him?"

"Can I ask why you want to meet with him?"

The woman's clipped tone made Ally uneasy. Did she already know that Ally was up to something?

"I just have a few questions for him."

"You can ask me. I'm sure I can answer anything business related, and likely personally as well. I'm his wife."

"Oh." Ally's voice dropped. She hadn't expected his wife to be the one answering the phone. "I met Scott at the party last night."

"The mayor's party?"

"Yes."

"And you're calling now because?"

"It's just that he seemed to know the deputy mayor personally."

"What business is that of yours?"

"It's not." Ally sighed and realized she'd just struck out. "It's not my business at all. Thanks for your time, Maddie." She hung up the phone and stared out through the windshield.

It was difficult to accept that she'd just blown her first lead. There was no way that either Scott or his wife would talk to her after that botched attempt to get an appointment. Of course there was always the option of breaking in and taking a look around their home. However, that was a huge risk to take for something that was just a hunch. She decided to investigate Scott a little more before doing something so risky.

Ally drove to the library and settled in front of one of the computers. As she sorted through all of the information she could find about Scott, she came across a newspaper article that showed him shaking hands with Mayor Malcolm. Mayor Malcolm looked quite pleased as he smiled for the camera. The reporter who wrote the article had a very poor opinion of the mayor, due to him selecting some service providers outside of Freely even though there were some viable providers from Freely.

Ally glanced at her phone and noticed it was almost lunch time. She gathered her things and drove back towards the shop. The moment that she saw the patrol car in the parking lot her heart skipped a beat. Had they arrived to arrest them? Ally parked and strode towards the door. When she heard voices she stopped and put her ear to the door to listen. She wanted to hear what the officer asked before she decided whether to sneak away or enter.

"It's pretty clear that someone at the dinner poisoned Julia. Since the tarts were the last thing that she ate and seem to have possibly caused her coughing fit, we of course tested them."

"And they came out clear, I'm sure."

"The problem is, we don't know if she consumed more than one. The remainder of the tart on her plate was clear, as were the rest of the tarts that we collected. However, that doesn't mean that one she ate earlier wasn't poisoned."

"All right Officer, if you're going to insist on considering me a suspect, please enlighten me as to my motive. I've lived and worked in this town all my life. What could I possibly gain from Julia's death?"

"I was hoping you would tell me that. From what I can tell you didn't have any issues with Julia."

"Of course I didn't. What I knew of the woman was that she was a good person, who worked hard to gain her position and took her job very seriously. Why would I have anything against someone like that?"

"Maybe, because you never had the chance to continue your political career."

"My what?" Charlotte laughed. "What are you talking about?"

"There was a time when you tried to create a new position, a neighborhood liaison to represent the small businesses in Blue River. My research showed that you were involved in several protests in an attempt to get the position created."

"Are you kidding?" She laughed again. "That was decades ago. It had nothing to do with Freely anyway. The truth is you have nothing to hold against me. There is no trace of poison in any of the tarts, and I have no motive."

"Maybe you don't, but what about your granddaughter, I haven't finished investigating her connection with Julia."

"There's nothing to investigate. I don't think

she had ever even met Julia. Ally had nothing to do with any of this."

"So you say, but maybe there are things about her that even you don't know. People can surprise us, you know."

"Sure, she surprises me all of the time, but not when it comes to something like this. Maybe instead of grasping at straws you should focus your investigation on people who were actual enemies of the deputy mayor. I'm sure she had a few."

"I can assure you everyone is being investigated."

"Good, now if you don't mind I have work to finish up."

"Just once more, can you tell me where you were when Julia died?"

"I told you already. I went to the restroom to freshen up before the speeches began. There was a line so it took me a little longer than expected."

"Huh. And your granddaughter, Ally, where

was she?"

"I was at the table with the tarts. The entire night." Ally shut the door behind her and set her jaw as the officer turned to face her.

"Ah, there you are. I have a few questions for you."

"No, you don't." Charlotte waved her hand through the air. "You've taken up enough of our time. Neither of us had anything to do with Julia's death. But I can promise you that her murderer is out there thinking he or she got away with it, while you stand here with absolutely no reason to question us."

"Fine." Officer Frank sighed and adjusted his hat. "I can see that you're not willing to cooperate. I'll make a note of that."

Ally raised an eyebrow. "Do you really think that intimidates me?"

"It should." He held her gaze. "I know about you and your connection with one of the detectives in Blue River. But he is not here, and he is not working the case, I am."

"I know that."

"Then why won't you answer my questions."

"I'm willing to answer any question you have, but my grandmother has already told you everything we know."

"Everything?" He put his hands on his hips. Ally took a breath.

"Okay, I did notice a man at the dinner who seemed to have something against Julia, and her husband. His name is Scott Brally. That's all I know."

"How do you know he had a problem with them?" Officer Frank made a note on his notepad.

"Because he told me. He also said he'd probably had too much to drink."

"Thank you. I will look into him. Did you notice anything else unusual that night?"

"No. Not at all." Ally frowned. "I wish I knew something more, I really do."

"Just do me a favor and keep the shop closed until we get this straightened out."

"Is that a request or a requirement?" Ally met his eyes.

"A requirement. It's for your own protection."

"We can't keep it closed indefinitely. Please hurry up and get this crime solved, Officer."

"I will." He tipped his hat and walked out of the shop. Ally rested her elbows on the counter beside her grandmother.

"Where's Luke when we need him?"

"Don't worry about it. He has no proof."

"But will he need any, if we have to keep the shop closed the rumor mills will be running out of control."

"Let them run. You and I both know that we've done nothing wrong." Charlotte wiped down the counter and did her best to look relaxed. "So, tell me what you found out about this man you told me about."

"I tried to get to speak to him, but I didn't

manage to. I bungled it when I called to speak to him at his work, I got his wife instead and didn't realize it. Now she's not going to be getting me any meeting with her husband, I can assure you. But I did find out that he owns a waste services company and that Mayor Malcolm is the one that gave him the contract for Freely. It is also the same company that services Blue River."

"Hm, that's interesting."

"I just hope that Officer Frank really does follow up on it," Ally said.

"He seems like an intelligent man. No Luke, of course, but he'll have to do. Would you mind giving me a lift home? I'd like to do a little networking and see if anyone has any insights as to who might be responsible for this."

"Sure." Ally held open the door for her. As she turned to leave she realized she hadn't locked the door. She turned back fast and locked it. Had she forgotten to lock it on the day that Julia was murdered?

Chapter Six

After dropping off her grandmother Ally headed back home. She was exhausted from the tension of the day and looked forward to a quiet evening and dinner. Before she cooked she settled on the couch to relax for a while. Peaches stretched across her stomach. Ally stroked her hand through Peaches' fur. As usual she began to relax the moment she felt the subtle vibration of Peaches' purr. More like her best friend than her pet, Peaches helped her get through the most difficult times in her life. As she waited for the rest of her body to relax she spoke softly to the cat.

"The police think that the tarts might have been poisoned, Peaches. I know it wasn't the tarts that did it, but still, I can't help feeling as if I could have done something to help." She sighed and scratched lightly behind Peaches' ear.

Ally stared through the window that overlooked the backyard. As she looked at the rustle of the leaves in the trees Julia crept into her thoughts. One moment she was smiling, the next she was gone. She couldn't do anything to change that, but there was one thing that she could do. She could find out the truth about what had happened to her. But how?

As determined as she was, she wasn't sure that she would be able to get any information. Peaches crawled in a slow circle around her lap. She settled once more and started to curl her tail around her body. Before she did she struck Ally on the nose with the fluffy tip of her tail. In that moment Ally remembered the napkin that struck her in the face. She remembered looking up to see the photographer with his camera pointed in her direction. She ducked him before he could take her picture. But he took pictures the entire night, especially of the mayor and the deputy mayor. Maybe he caught something on camera, such as a hand slipping poison into Julia's food, or someone glaring from a distance. He might not even know that he did. If she had a chance to look at those pictures she might be lucky enough to solve the murder right away.

"Thank you, as always, Peaches." She leaned down and kissed the top of the cat's head. One glance at the clock told her that she might still be able to catch the photographer at the newspaper office. She grabbed her purse and a box of chocolates, and headed out the door. When she arrived at the newspaper office the sign on the door was turned to 'closed', but she noticed lights on inside. She took a moment to run her fingers through her long hair, then knocked hard on the door. A moment later she saw a shadow in the window beside the door. As the person approached she could tell that it was the photographer from his tall and lanky frame, as well as the long goatee that grew from his chin. She knocked again, a bit harder. He stood beside the door as if trying to decide whether to open it. Ally put on her sweetest smile and tipped her head towards the door.

"Hello? Is someone there?" The doorknob twisted, then the door swung open. "We're closed." He gazed at her with dark, impenetrable eyes. She had hoped a bit of chocolate would do the trick. But when she looked into his eyes she remembered that he hadn't eaten the tart at the party because it was chocolate, so she doubted that the chocolate would persuade him to do anything, but it was still worth a try.

"I'm here to see you." She held his gaze. "I just need a few minutes of your time, please."

"My time? Why?" He narrowed his eyes.

"I brought you some chocolate." She held out the box to him and lifted the lid so that the smell of the chocolate would waft towards him.

"I'm allergic to chocolate." He pursed his lips.

"Oh, I'm sorry." She closed the box and tucked it under her arm. "That must be terrible."

"It's not exactly tragic." He sighed and glanced at his watch. "What is this about? I'm working on a project and would rather not be distracted."

"Listen, I know you took the pictures at the

cocktail party the night the deputy mayor died."

"So?" He leaned against the doorway. "What does that matter?"

"I hoped that you might let me take a look at them? I'd just like to see if maybe there's something there that no one noticed."

"Oh, you mean the pictures that I've been told not to publish?" He chuckled. "Who are you again?"

"My name is Ally. I run Charlotte's Chocolate Heaven in Blue River. I guess you haven't been there before."

"No, I haven't. But I remember you from the party." His gaze lingered on her for a moment. "Still, I can't show you or anyone else the pictures."

"But I'm not going to publish them, I'm just going to look at them. That's not a crime is it?" She smiled again.

"Oh sure, don't worry about me losing my job or anything like that, as long as you get your

71

murder fix."

"My what?" Her eyes widened.

"Look, I've seen your kind before. You're a murder junkie. You want to know everything there is to know about a crime that has nothing to do with you. I don't think that's any reason to risk my job."

"I'm not a murder junkie." She crossed her arms and studied him with annoyance. "I mean, I do want to solve the crime, but not for any other reason than making sure that Julia gets justice."

"Right, and none of the fame that will come from solving the murder?"

"Right, none of that." She frowned. "You don't have to believe me, but I can assure you that my only interest is in making sure that whoever did this to Julia pays for it."

"Why? Were you friends?" He stepped back from the door some. Ally took it as an invitation to step inside. As she did she shook her head.

"No, we weren't friends. I didn't know her

very well. This will probably sound foolish to you, but I just keep seeing her smile. It was just so radiant." She sighed and shook her head. "One moment she was there, the next she was gone. I have to make sure that justice is served." She braced herself. Would he tell her to leave? Would he laugh in her face?

"She did have a beautiful smile." He lowered his eyes. "And a beautiful laugh."

"You noticed?"

"It's hard not to when you're the one taking the pictures." He shrugged. "I get to see all of the little details that most people miss out on."

"That's all I'm asking to see, some little details. I'm not going to put your job at risk. But if you let me just take a quick look, then I might be able to figure some things out."

"Honestly, I have no idea why I'm doing this. But, fine..." He stepped aside and gestured to an office not far from the door. "I hate to think of never seeing that beautiful smile again. So, if you think you can do something to bring her murderer to justice, then go ahead and try. But you can't let any of this come back on me."

"I won't. I promise." Ally's body relaxed with relief. She settled into an office chair in front of the desk and peered at the photographs spread out before her. There were many more than she had anticipated. To look at the fine details that she wanted to could take hours.

"Are you sure I can't take copies of these home to look at?"

"Absolutely not." He shook his head. "Isn't it enough that I let you in here to look at them?"

"Yes, it is. It's just that there are so many, I'm not sure where to start."

"If it were me, I would start from the end of the story and work my way back. It's how I select the photographs that I publish. That way I don't miss any important moments in the story."

"Oh, good idea." She glanced up at him then looked back down at the pictures. "Then, I guess I should start at the time of death and work back from there."

"I stopped taking pictures when she collapsed." He pointed to a picture in the pile. "That's the last one I took of her before she died." He showed her the picture as his cell phone began to ring. "Ralph speaking," he said as he picked it up. He lowered his voice and walked with his phone to another room.

She studied the picture for any sign of what might have poisoned Julia.

All she saw was Julia eagerly speaking into the microphone. When she shifted her attention to the next picture she noticed that in her hand was a champagne flute and she was drinking from it when Ralph snapped the picture. Ally's heart dropped. Was that it? The glass of champagne? She didn't think it could be that simple, but there it was. The last thing that the deputy mayor drank. Maybe her coughing fit had nothing to do with the poison. The coughing could have been random, and the champagne could have easily contained the poison. Ally looked to see if Ralph was back.

When she couldn't see him she quickly took out her cell phone and snapped photos of the last few photographs. She stopped when she heard Ralph's footsteps approaching. She quickly put away her phone just before Ralph entered through the doorway. He was still on his phone.

Ally narrowed her eyes as she looked at the photograph of Julia holding the glass of champagne. She then looked at the photo of the glass on the podium. She studied the glass of champagne. Something stood out about it, but she couldn't quite place what. She moved on to the picture prior to that one. The photograph captured the moment that Mayor Malcolm handed the deputy mayor the glass of champagne. With both the mayor's and Julia's hand on the glass, the picture itself was powerful. She looked at the picture taken before it and she could see the mayor picking up both his and Julia's champagne glass. She looked back to the picture of him handing her the glass. He handed the one to her from his right hand.

Ally then looked back to the picture of him picking up the champagne glasses. The one he had picked up in his right hand was his glass. He had handed her his glass of champagne. Was that deliberate or accidental? If the champagne was poisoned then was the poison meant for the mayor? Or was he the one that had poisoned it and then given it to Julia? If the champagne was poisoned then Mayor Malcolm was her main suspect. He could have easily dropped poison in his own glass before handing it to Julia. But why would he want the deputy mayor dead?

Chapter Seven

Early the next morning Ally called her grandmother. She answered in her cheerful tone as if she'd been awake for hours.

"How are you this morning, Ally?"

"I thought I might wake you."

"Oh no, you know I'm always up early. Want to come over for breakfast? I made muffins."

"Yes, that sounds great. I'll be there in fifteen minutes."

"I'll put on some coffee."

Ally hung up the phone and hurried to feed the animals. Arnold looked up at her with eager eyes.

"Don't worry, the food is coming." She reached for the bag under the counter, and filled Arnold's dish to the brim. "I know I haven't spent much time with you, buddy. I promise tonight, I will take you for a nice, long walk. Okay?" She massaged his ears. Peaches yowled as she walked into the kitchen.

"Yes, yes, you're next." Once the animals were settled she drove over to Freely Lakes. Her grandmother waited with a large blueberry muffin and fresh coffee.

"This is just what I want to see, thank you so much."

"Anything for you, darling. I have some news for you."

"Me too."

"Okay, you first. What is it?"

"The last person to give Julia anything to eat or drink was the mayor."

"Really?" Charlotte's eyes widened. "How do you know?"

"I remembered the photographer taking pictures of the event. So I went to see him and I managed to get him to let me look at the pictures. One of the last photographs of Julia alive includes Mayor Malcolm handing her the glass of champagne for the toast. It looks like it was his glass."

"Oh no." Charlotte gasped. "My news is that the police cleared us. They traced the poison to her champagne glass on the podium. There was no poison found in any other champagne or glass. So they think that either the champagne was poisoned once it was in the glass or the actual glass had the poison put in it before the champagne was added."

"Wouldn't someone have noticed it?" Ally's eyes widened.

"That was exactly what I asked Officer Frank. But apparently it could have gone unnoticed. The poison used can come as a clear, thin liquid that sticks to the glass like oil and is very difficult to see unless you're specifically looking for it."

"Interesting."

"So either Mayor Malcolm poisoned the champagne and handed it to Julia or the glass was poisoned."

"Maybe the poison was intended for Mayor Malcolm, it was his glass after all." Ally showed her grandmother the pictures of the mayor handing Julia the glass to explain what she was talking about.

"Yes, that's possible. I prefer that option. I don't think I could believe that the mayor would kill her."

"Why not?"

"It's just that, he's the mayor, if he wanted to kill her, why would he do it so publicly?" Charlotte asked.

"Maybe he got some twisted satisfaction from that." Ally frowned. "Murderers sometimes have strange desires."

"Maybe, but still. A powerful man like him, could handle things behind the scenes."

"True. He could have thought that a public death like that might make people less suspicious of him."

"It's possible. There's only one way to know

for sure. Just because he handed her the champagne glass, that still isn't proof that he poisoned her. It seems likely that he was the intended victim," Charlotte said. "I doubt that the police are going to be in any rush to arrest him without solid evidence."

"You're probably right."

"I think you need to try to talk to him."

"But how will I get to talk to him?" Ally asked.

"You'll think of a way. You're pretty creative." Charlotte smiled and met Ally's eyes. "You just need to think outside the box. Try to see what you can find out without antagonizing him."

"That's easier said than done."

"I'm sure there's a way we can get some information from him. I'll tell you what, I'll run the shop today and you see what you can find out at the mayor's office. My face is more well-known around there so I think it's better if you try rather than me."

"All right, I'll give it my best shot. Maybe I

should take some delicious treats with me. That opens a lot of doors."

"Indeed, it does. We can put together a box to leave at the office."

"Perfect."

"Also, Julia's memorial is on Thursday. I think we should both be there."

"I agree."

"It's good for the broader community to show respect. Her poor husband is going to have a lot to deal with."

Ally bit her tongue as she recalled the hateful way that Scott Brally had talked about Julia's marriage. She didn't feel the need to revisit that conversation. Maybe Scott was just bitter with his own life. Either way Julia's husband was now a widower and he would need support. Ally left Freely Lakes and drove towards the mayor's office. In her mind she rehearsed all of the ways she might be able to get inside. However, each plan had a weakness that she didn't like.

When Ally arrived she pretended that she had a delivery of chocolates, which she sometimes did, for someone in the building. A familiar security guard let her through security to the floor the mayor's office was on. The anticipation of speaking to the mayor had her nerves on edge. She was sure that he would have no time for her. As she walked towards the receptionist's desk she heard some raised voices from behind the office door. The desk was unmanned. Ally waited until she was sure there was no one watching, then crept up to the door. Even though it was just open a crack, the voices inside were raised loud enough that she could hear the words clearly.

"I don't have to put up with this." The female voice raised.

Ally jumped as she heard something crash to the floor inside the office. "Don't push me right now, Martha. My temper is already on edge."

"I'm not afraid of you, Tim. I know you want me to be, but I'm not. I never have been, and I never will be. I'm a strong person, that's what you didn't realize when you married me. You thought you'd get a pretty face that you could intimidate into serving your every whim, but that is not who I am. If someone crosses me they pay, and that includes you."

"I am the mayor, don't you realize what havoc I can cause in your life?"

"I'm not afraid. I don't depend on you for anything. You're the one that's depending on me, Tim. How will it look when the newspapers print that you killed your lover? How is that going to play at election time?"

"No one is going to print that."

"Everyone is waiting to print that. I've had calls from every reporter in town. All I have to do is say the word and they will print exactly what I just said."

"But it isn't true."

"You say it isn't. That doesn't make it untrue. You lie for a living, Tim, why do you think people are going to believe you?"

"It isn't true!" He shouted. Ally took a step back from the door and held her breath for a moment. "Julia was a good woman, she was a good friend. You have been after me for years about our friendship, but that's all it ever was, friendship. I don't care what the public thinks."

"Well, you need to care. Because, when the media gets hold of this, they're going to have it plastered all over the country, with me, the idiot wife, pictured right beside you."

"You believe me don't you?"

"What does it matter?" Her laughter trickled out of the office. "If it wasn't Julia it was any one of your other conquests. At least if it was Julia, I would have a little more faith in your taste in women. Why do you care if I believe you or not?"

"Martha, please. You have to think about what you're saying."

"Oh, that's it, right? You don't actually care, you just want me to tell you that I'll lie to the police for you, that I'll have your back like I always do. Don't think for a second that I will do anything to jeopardize your position. You may be the mayor in title, but I worked just as hard to get here. All I want is this scandal swept under the rug. Figure it out."

Chapter Eight

Charlotte didn't have to wait long for the shop to get its first three customers. She expected her usual visitors, especially with all of the gossip spreading through town. She set out a sample tray and smiled as the three women dug right in.

"Enjoy. You three are some of my best customers."

"Or we're addicted." Mrs. Bing laughed.

"There could be much worse things to be addicted to." Mrs. White smiled and popped a chocolate into her mouth.

"Yes, mm." Mrs. Cale couldn't quite speak around the chocolate she was eating.

Charlotte leaned against the counter and studied the three women. "Did you hear?"

It was all she needed to say to launch a torrid of information.

"Oh, yes of course, I found out right after it

happened." Mrs. Bing sighed and shook her head. "What a terrible, terrible tragedy. I don't think Julia even had a chance to have any children, did she?"

"No, but not every woman wants children. Besides, maybe she was worried about the DNA test results." Mrs. Cale wiggled her eyebrows.

"Now, now, let's not talk ill of the dead." Mrs. White frowned.

"It's not talking ill, it's just discussing her life." Mrs. Cale looked over at Charlotte. "The poor thing was caught up in a sordid affair that she would never have gotten free from. The man she loved, was already married."

"Oh really?" Charlotte clucked her tongue. "I didn't know she was having an affair with anyone."

"Well, she most certainly was." Mrs. Bing whistled.

"Girls, at least tell the whole story if you're going to tell it at all." Mrs. White took a deep breath. "The rumor is that Julia and Mayor Malcolm have been having an affair for many years. Apparently, they were once caught in a compromising position at work."

"Wow." Charlotte's eyes widened. "I never even suspected it. I wonder what the mayor's wife thinks of all of this? Not to mention Julia's husband?"

"Martha is clueless. At least she was for a long time. Maybe she found out the truth." Mrs. Cale pursed her lips.

"You think she might have done it?" Mrs. Bing popped another chocolate into her mouth and bit down on it.

"It's an awful thing to think." Mrs. White looked down at the counter. "But a lover's quarrel can be a very volatile situation."

"Everyone seemed so calm at the party though. Mayor Malcolm was polite to Julia, and Martha hung on his arm as if she adored him," Charlotte said.

"Politicians." Mrs. White rolled her eyes. "The one thing they're good at is telling lies and wearing masks."

"Maybe so, maybe so." Charlotte refilled the sample tray. "It would be motive, that's for sure. I wonder if the police know about it."

"If they don't know yet, they will soon. That chatty secretary is the reason the rumor got started in the first place." Mrs. Bing helped herself to some of the new samples.

"Donna Jenkins?" Charlotte asked. Charlotte knew her quite well because she was a regular at the chocolate shop.

"Yes, that's her. She talks and talks. If you get her started it's nearly impossible to get her to stop. Charlotte, can I get a little box of these hazelnut clusters please?"

"Of course." Charlotte got a small box for Mrs. Bing.

"How much?" Mrs. Bing asked as she picked up a milk caramel.

"On the house!" Charlotte smiled. The three woman would buy a lot of chocolates and Charlotte liked to occasionally give them some to take home for free. They often recommended the shop so she made the money back many times over.

"Thank you," Mrs. Bing said.

Charlotte watched as the women continued to sample as many of the chocolates on the tray as they could. While the women were occupied with the chocolates Charlotte excused herself and picked up her cell phone. She texted a message to Ally.

Talk to Donna Jenkins if you have the chance. Find out about a possible affair between Mayor Malcolm and Julia.

***

Ally's phone chimed with an alert that she had received a new text. She ducked away from the door. With the level of the voices inside she hoped the chime was drowned out. She read the text and raised an eyebrow. The secretary, Donna Jenkins, returned to her desk as Ally walked up to it. She held a coffee in her hand as she sat down.

"Hello there." Ally smiled. The woman looked up at her with furrowed brows. Ally assumed she had overheard part of the argument as well. "These are for you." She set down the box on the desk.

"Hi Ally. What is it?" She looked towards the box with interest.

"Just an assortment of chocolates from the best chocolate shop around."

"There's only one." She smiled.

"They're for you, Donna, and whoever you might want to share them with."

"What's the catch?" Donna lifted the top of the box and peeked inside.

"I'd like a few minutes with the mayor."

"Oh, you and one hundred other people." Donna shook her head. "I'm sorry it's going to take more than a box of candy to get that."

Ally frowned. "Well, then maybe you could

answer a few questions for me?"

"Depends on what they are." She drew the box close to her. Ally smiled as she considered that as an acceptance of the offer.

"I'm a little concerned with something that I overheard."

"Oh? The argument? That happens quite a bit."

"No, not that. One of my customers mentioned that the mayor is considered a suspect in the deputy mayor's murder. When I heard that, I was shocked."

"Well, you should be. Whoever told you that has the wrong information. There's no way that Mayor Malcolm had anything to do with Julia's death."

"You would certainly know. I'm sure that you know him better than most people ever could."

Donna's cheeks flushed. "Yes, that's true. People don't realize how much a secretary does to support the career of the individual they work for."

"I do." Ally rested her hands on the desk and leaned closer to her. "So tell me, Donna, do you have any idea who might have done this to Julia?"

Donna pursed her lips. Ally held her breath as she wondered whether the woman would share anything with her. Then Donna nodded.

"All right, between us, I'm certain of who the killer is."

"Really?" Ally fixed her gaze to Donna's. "Who?"

"This is the situation. The mayor is reviewing all of the services contracts for the area, including waste disposal. There's a lot of pressure from voters to make everything as local as possible. So he has to choose a new provider for waste disposal. Now the current provider, Garbage Inc., has been providing service to this town for a few years. This town, and Blue River, are the only ones they service. So, if the mayor pulled the plug on the contract, Garbage Inc. would likely go out of business. I think that the owner is the one who did it."

"That's a bit extreme don't you think? To murder over a contract?"

"Not if you knew this man. Scott Brally. He's a fierce guy. A real bully. I don't even like to be alone in the same room with him. He's only kept the contract for so long because of his bullying tactics. I don't think he would let go of the contract easily."

"Did you tell the police this?" Ally's heart skipped a beat. Did she really make fun of the deputy mayor with her killer?

"Of course I did. But they kept asking me questions about the mayor. So I told them to arrest me if they wanted to ask me questions, otherwise they had to leave the office."

Ally couldn't help but smile. Donna had plenty of nerve. She was relieved that the woman was willing to tell her anything.

"Did you ever notice anyone else who might have had problems with Julia? I mean, why would

Scott target her instead of the mayor?"

"I don't know for sure, other than the termination of a contract requires both of their signatures. Maybe he thought Julia was the easier target. As for enemies, the mayor has a few of them, but I think they are mostly harmless."

"Have you heard anything from Scott Brally recently?"

"I didn't have to hear anything. He was at the cocktail party the night of Julia's death."

Ally nodded. "I see."

"Yes, I saw him and his wife the moment they came in."

"Did you see him go near Julia?"

"No. Honestly, once I saw him I did my best to avoid him. Now I wish I had paid more attention."

Ally glanced towards the mayor's office. She wished she could get inside to ask him some questions, but she knew it was too much of a risk to push Donna. Instead she decided to take a chance and ask a question that might upset her.

"Someone mentioned to me that perhaps Julia and the mayor had something more than a business relationship?" She didn't want to mention that she had just overheard the mayor and his wife fighting about it as that might put Donna on the defensive if she knew that she had been listening so closely.

"Ha." Donna narrowed her eyes. "No one can mind their own business these days, can they?"

"So, it's true?"

"Whether it's true or not, it's no one's business. What a man does behind closed doors is off limits. Don't you think?"

Ally took a deep breath. "Maybe it depends on the situation."

"Well, in my book, asking questions like that is an invasion of privacy. Not something that I will participate in. So if you want dirt, you need to dig somewhere else."

"I'm sorry, Donna. I just want to find out who

killed Julia."

"I understand. But I have nothing more to tell."

"You've helped a lot already. I hope you enjoy the chocolates."

"Oh, I intend to." She grinned.

Just as Ally turned to walk out of the office, Mrs. Malcolm pushed the inner office door open and stomped past her.

"Mrs. Malcolm, would you like me to call you a car?" Donna stood up half-way from her chair.

"Yes please. He gets the office, the least I can get is a nice car." She continued walking.

Ally hurried to catch up with her. Before the elevator doors could close she ducked inside with Mrs. Malcolm. A grimace that flickered across her face warned her that she didn't want company.

"Men, right?" Ally rolled her eyes.

"Excuse me?"

"Oh, I'm sorry. I overheard you and your

husband fighting. I just thought you could use a sympathetic ear."

"Ha. What are you, a reporter?" She scowled across the elevator.

"No, I manage a chocolate shop. I just know what it's like to have the person you care for the most turn against you." She balled her hands into fists at her sides. "It just makes you want to lose your temper, doesn't it?"

"I don't know what you're talking about. My husband and I have our moments, but that's because his position is so stressful. It's not easy to have so much responsibility. Sometimes he needs to blow off some steam. I don't resent him for that."

"Oh." Ally shrugged. "I guess I misunderstood."

"Yes, you did. In fact, it might be better if you stayed out of other people's business in the future. If it doesn't involve you, then it doesn't concern you." She jabbed her finger against one of the elevator buttons. The doors slid open and she walked out. Ally thought about following her, but she assumed that she wouldn't get any more information out of her. Instead she continued down in the elevator until it reached the bottom.

When Ally stepped out of the elevator she found a small crowd in the lobby. It only took her a moment to recognize that it was reporters. The mayor's wife stepped out from a door that lead to the staircase and several of the reporters shoved their microphones in her face. She waved them away as she tried to get past them. A photographer lunged forward in an attempt to get a picture. Ally recognized him right away. After Mrs. Malcolm left, Ally walked up to Ralph.

"Hey, what are you trying to get a picture of?"

"You again?" He frowned. "What now?"

"I'm just curious, what's the big story around Mrs. Malcolm?"

"The big story is that she's become one of the prime suspects in the deputy mayor's murder."

"Why is that?"

He slipped his camera strap over his shoulder. "Rumors of an affair, lots of reports of loud fights, she and Julia even got into it once at a barbecue."

"I hadn't heard that. What happened?"

"Martha had a few too many, called her some terrible names, and demanded she admit to the affair."

"And?" Ally leaned closer to him.

"And, she didn't admit to it. Either she was sober enough not to, or there was nothing to admit."

"You're the one with an eye for detail. What do you think?"

He scrunched up his nose and then lifted the camera to his eye. Ally shifted from one foot to the other as he stared at her through the lens. Then he lowered the camera and nodded.

"I think that a man like Mayor Malcolm can have any woman he wants. I've followed Julia's career, and I've followed Mayor Malcolm's career.

Never once have I caught them in a romantic interlude. That tells me that either they're very good at hiding it, or there is nothing to catch."

"Still not an answer." Ally crossed her arms.

"There are no answers in life, sweetheart, just assumptions and intentions."

Ally considered his words. She watched as Martha's car drove away. If the affair between Julia and Mayor Malcolm actually took place the mayor's wife had motive. Julia's own husband had motive. If Julia was threatening to make the affair public the mayor had plenty of motive as well. But there was one person who weighed heavily on her mind. There was no avoiding it anymore, she needed to look into Scott's eyes to try to figure out if he was involved in Julia's death. In the back of her mind she could hear Luke warning her not to take such a risk, but just as she would have if he were there to give the advice, she ignored it.

Chapter Nine

Instead of calling ahead Ally drove straight to the address that was still stored in her phone. When she arrived at the business, she noticed that it was a small rectangular building. For some reason she expected it to be larger. She took a deep breath and braced herself for the argument that would ensue. However, when she stepped inside she did her best to put on a sunny smile. She hoped that Scott's wife wouldn't recognize her when she walked up to the reception desk.

"Hi there."

"Hi?" The receptionist looked up at her with a raised eyebrow. She was not the person that had been at the cocktail party with Scott. She was quite young, probably still in her teens.

"Do you think I could get a minute with Scott?"

"Why?" She chomped on a piece of gum.

"We're just old friends. I just want a minute of

his time."

"Let me check." She snapped her gum and picked up the phone. She uttered a few quiet words then hung up the phone. "Mr. Brally will see you now."

"Great." Ally walked towards the door of the office. She couldn't help but notice that the door frame was created out of recycled material. Her mind wandered off as she considered the amount of things that could be made from everything she threw away.

"Hello?" The voice boomed and drew her attention.

"Hi." She smiled at the man who stood up from behind his desk. Despite his loud voice he had a friendly smile on his face. She held his gaze as she sat down across from him. "Thanks so much for agreeing to see me."

"Old friends? If I'm not mistaken we barely even met." He narrowed his eyes.

"You're right. I'm sorry, I just needed a chance

to speak with you."

"Is this about Julia?'

"Yes, it is."

"Then I think your time is better spent with the police. I don't have anything to say about it."

"You didn't exactly hide your feelings about her."

"I was drunk and making stupid comments. There's nothing to it. So why are you really here?"

"Honestly, I just wanted to get your side of things."

"My side of things?" Scott asked.

Ally sat back in her chair and sighed. "Operating a small business in a small town means I hear just about every rumor that flies around. Lately I've been hearing quite a few about you."

He shifted in his chair. His shoulders lifted and his jaw tightened. His entire demeanor changed so suddenly that it shocked Ally.

"Oh? What have you heard about me?"

"Just that you are pretty tough to deal with sometimes. And perhaps you had a bone to pick with the deputy mayor."

He stood up from his chair. Her heart lurched and she slouched back in her chair. As he rounded the desk her eyes widened. Would he hurt her? The flash of heat in his eyes indicated that he might. As she stared at him he met her gaze with a stern tension in his expression.

"Did you come here to accuse me of murder?"

"I didn't say that."

"You don't have to. I know how to read a situation. Clearly, the only reason you wanted this meeting was because you suspect me. I'm honestly disappointed."

"I've already told you, Mr. Brally, I came here to hear your side. I didn't say that I believed any of these rumors, just that I've heard them. In my experience the best way to find the truth is to go to the source, so that's what I did. I'm sure you can appreciate that."

"I can, but I'd prefer that you automatically grasped that I would never be involved in such a thing."

"Never? What about the rumors I've heard about you intimidating people?" She stared him straight in the eyes. His lips tightened, then curved into a smirk. He leaned back against the desk right in front of her.

"So, after hearing the things you did about me it didn't give you the idea to avoid me?"

"I'm not easily frightened. I'm sure what I heard is partly false and exaggerated. Am I wrong?"

"It doesn't matter what's true and what's not. All that matters is that I had nothing to do with Julia's death. So, you're in the wrong place."

"I'd like to believe that."

"Then do." He narrowed his eyes.

"What if I tell the police what you told me?" She stared back at him. "About how you wanted to shake things up a little bit."

His nostrils flared. "You go right ahead and do that. It won't lead to anything, because there's nothing to find. Now get out of my office."

Ally stood up from the chair. She didn't wait to be asked twice. As she hurried out of the office she heard his voice boom behind her.

"Kristy, you are so close to being fired! Use your brain once in a while!" He slammed the door to his office. Ally rushed outside to her car. Had she just antagonized a dangerous man? She wondered what the consequences might be.

Chapter Ten

On the drive to Freely Lakes Ally's heart continued to pound. The memory of the anger in Scott's eyes was intense. The fairly friendly man she'd met over chocolate tarts at the cocktail party was not the man she saw in that office. There was no doubt in her mind that he could be involved in Julia's death. She parked and walked up to her grandmother's apartment.

"Ally, I was worried about you. What have you been up to?"

"I went to see Scott Brally."

"Alone?" Charlotte asked.

"Yes."

"I wish you hadn't gone there alone. What did you find out from him?"

"The only thing I found out is that Scott Brally has a temper, and he has no problem with showing it."

"So, what next?" Charlotte frowned.

"Here's the problem." Ally sighed. "We've got Mayor Malcolm, his wife, and Scott Brally, all of them look good for it."

"But it was Mayor Malcolm that gave her the poisoned glass of champagne."

"Yes, maybe that's the key to figuring all of this out." Ally pulled out her cell phone and looked through the pictures that she had taken of Ralph's photos. She looked at the one with the champagne glass on the podium. "There's something about this picture that has been bothering me. Something is off about it." Ally scanned through the photos that she had.

"What?" Charlotte leaned close.

"I'm not sure, yet." Ally shook her head, then she tried to relax as she looked at the glass on the podium. "It's the glass!" Ally jumped so fast that she almost dropped her phone.

"What?" Charlotte looked over at her. "What do you mean?"

"I knew there was something off about this picture. I knew it." Ally displayed the picture of the champagne glass on the podium. "The glass, it's different from all the other glasses that were used that night. It has a diamond pattern etched into the glass."

"How can you know that for sure? They might have used one set of glasses for the general public and one for the important politicians."

"No, I checked through the other photographs. All of the glasses that I saw were the same. So, why was this different glass there?"

"Hm. That's a good question." Charlotte narrowed her eyes. "Maybe the person giving the speeches gets a different glass."

"I thought of that but this was Mayor Malcolm's glass not Julia's."

"Maybe the mayor got a special glass because he's the mayor."

"It's possible. But what if the murderer brought it in from outside."

"If they laced the glass with the poison before they brought it in it would make the murder well-planned and deliberate," Charlotte said.

"Exactly." Ally flipped through the few photographs she had managed to take snaps of on her phone. "The mayor is the one that handed her the glass. Maybe he brought it from his own stash. Maybe it was too difficult to poison a glass at the party, so he had to bring it with him."

"Well, if he did bring the glass in that would mean that he could have laced it with poison before the dinner even began. No risk of someone seeing him do it. But, it's still a huge risk to his career and his freedom to kill Julia at all. It's still very likely that someone else brought it in from outside and it was intended for the mayor."

"Don't you see though?" Ally pointed to the picture of the glass again. "This is our smoking gun. If we can find a glass that matches this one, then we'll know where the glass came from, and have a good idea of who the murderer is."

"If it didn't come directly from the kitchen."

Charlotte raised an eyebrow. "It is possible that they ran out of glasses or a glass used in the main restaurant got mixed in with the ones used for private parties. It's easy to go down a road of assumptions, but we need to be sure that if it was the mayor that poisoned the glass and deliberately gave it to Julia that we have proof before we make any accusations."

"Well, there's only one way to do that."

"Ally?"

"Look, I tried to get into Mayor Malcolm's office once and failed. There's no way that I'm going to get into his home. But I do think I could get a quick look around his office after hours."

"That is a huge risk."

"I know." Ally frowned and tapped a fingertip along the table top. "But we don't have much choice. This is the type of man that will get away with murder if we're not careful. We need to find a way to get undeniable evidence, and that means taking the big risks."

"Ally, you're talking about the mayor's office. No." Charlotte stood up from the table. "No, absolutely not."

Ally looked up at her with a furrowed brow. "Mee-Maw, you have to let me grow up sometime."

"I let you grow up when you moved away and married that, ugh." She rolled her eyes. "No, not again."

"That was different."

"No, it wasn't." Charlotte put her hands on her hips. "I knew he wasn't good enough for you. I knew he was going to hurt you, but I kept it to myself. I thought it was more important to let you make your own choices, and I hoped that I was wrong. But I've regretted it every day since. You can't imagine how I'll feel if you end up in jail."

Ally sighed and rubbed a hand along her forehead. "Mee-Maw, I know you mean well, but this is important."

"It is, but you don't have to risk so much,

Ally."

"Mee-Maw, I'll be fine."

"Don't do anything to get yourself into trouble." Charlotte met her eyes. "And if you need my help let me know. I have a trick or two up my sleeve."

"Of course, Mee-Maw, I'll call you tonight." Ally turned and left the apartment. She couldn't let her grandmother put herself at risk, at the same time, she had to do what she thought was right. It was too late to do anything that night so she decided she would go home and have a good rest and decide what to do tomorrow.

Chapter Eleven

Ally spent the next day at the shop. Her grandmother was taking the day off to spend it with the social committee at Freely Lakes preparing for a movie night.

The day at the shop was busy and there were several customers. Ally kept herself occupied between customers by preparing a tray for an upcoming party as well as arranging some gift baskets. She tried to convince herself that it was a good thing the shop was cleared, and that in time Julia would have her justice. But the more she overheard the chatter in the shop, the more concerned she became.

"Even if he did do it, we'll never know." Mrs. Thompson from the laundromat uttered those words as she purchased a box of chocolates. The man beside her grunted.

"You're right about that. It'll be one more thing swept under the rug." He shook his head. "I can't say it surprises me, politics is a dirty game."

"Only if the players are." The two walked out of the shop together. A few hours later some high school students arrived to take advantage of the student discount. As Ally handed them their order, one of the girls in the group rolled her eyes as she looked at her phone.

"Can you believe this? They still haven't made an arrest. It's been all over the news."

"Do they know who did it?" One of the boys peered over her shoulder.

"Everyone thinks it was the mayor, but no one is making a move on the man."

"Who would?" He shook his head. "Just your average American corruption."

It struck Ally that these young teens were even more cynical than she was about the chances of Mayor Malcolm being arrested if he was found to be the murderer. She couldn't allow that.

By the time Ally closed up the shop she was determined to find out the truth, no matter what risk she had to take. She headed home to get some supplies and to feed Peaches and Arnold. The moment that Peaches jumped up onto the counter to wait for her food, Ally noticed the way that she stared at her.

"Don't start, Peaches. This is something that needs to be done. I'll be just fine." Peaches flicked her tail back and forth in a sharp warning motion. "Stop. Mee-Maw already gave me the lecture. Someone has to be willing to stand up to this man, and apparently that has to be me." She added a little extra food to Peaches' dish just in case she ended up in handcuffs. Then she tended to Arnold.

Ally changed into black clothes and sneakers, grabbed a flashlight, and headed right back out the door. The best thing was not to stop to think about it, if she did she might change her mind. When she parked outside the building that housed the mayor's office, she wondered how she was going to get past security.

Ally's best idea was to create a diversion. She

noticed that there was a floodlight not far from the entrance to the building. As she expected it was triggered by a motion sensor. She thought about it for a moment, then smiled. When she rummaged in the trunk she knew exactly what she was looking for. It was a cat toy she'd purchased for Peaches and intended to give to a charity as it was the most annoying thing she'd ever bought. A big fluffy gray mouse. It wound up and rolled across the floor, when it hit a wall or a piece of furniture it would change direction and continue to roll.

In the store Ally thought this would be an amazing toy that would save her from hours of bobbing a mouse on a stick for Peaches to chase. However, once the mouse got started, she discovered how frustrating it was. Wherever she walked that mouse managed to be under her feet. In the middle of the night, when nothing should have been moving in the house, the mouse would begin whirring and bumping into things. Even worse, Peaches didn't want anything to do with it, however Arnold was enamored. He barreled after the mouse every time he saw it. Arnold, much less graceful than Peaches, also bumped into things and knocked them over.

It wasn't until Ally took the mouse away that she finally got some decent sleep again. Now she hoped that it would be as effective on concrete. She wound it up and set it between two parking blocks near the floodlight. As she had hoped, the mouse triggered the light every time it rolled past. Since it just changed direction and continued back and forth, the light began to flicker on and off every fifteen seconds or so. The rest of the parking lot was dark, so the flood light drew a lot of attention. She hurried to the front door of the building and ducked into the shadows created by the canopy over the door.

After a few minutes a security guard came to the door. Ally held her breath as she wondered if he'd take the bait. When he stepped all the way out, Ally slipped her foot inside the door to keep it open. Once he was far enough away, she inched the door open and squeezed inside. The door fell shut behind her. She ran for the elevator and hoped that he would be occupied long enough not to notice that the elevator was in use.

When Ally reached the right floor she stepped out of the elevator and flattened herself against the wall. She began to move towards the office when her phone chimed. She nearly jumped out of her skin in reaction to the sound within the silent hallway. As quickly as she could she turned her phone off, then continued down the hall. As long as the security guard wasn't suspicious that someone might have broken in, she didn't think he would come up to check on the office.

When she reached the office she turned the knob. She was surprised that it was open. She carefully pushed the door open and peered around the reception area, but no one was there. When she tried the knob on the door that lead to the mayor's office, as she had expected it didn't budge. She looked at the receptionist's desk and decided to see if she could find a key.

She quietly rummaged through the drawers, but there was no sign of the key. By the time she had reached the bottom drawer she had given up hope. As she ran her hand over the contents of the bottom drawer her hand touched what felt like a key. She slowly pulled it out of the drawer. Could this really be it?

She walked over to the door and inserted the key. She almost squealed with excitement when the key turned and the door popped open.

Her heart raced as she wondered if an alarm would go off, or a security guard would come around the corner. Once she was sure that neither would happen she closed the door behind her. From her pocket she pulled out a flashlight and shone it around the office. When the light reflected off a glass, she froze. As quietly as she could she walked over to it. The flashlight beam danced along the thin, diamond pattern that encircled the midsection of the glass. It was the same diamond pattern that she had noticed on the glass in the photograph. It was a water glass not a champagne glass, but it was definitely the same pattern. Was it just a coincidence?

Ally's breath grew shallow as she reached out to pick it up. Just before she touched it, she stopped. What would she do with it? Would she steal it as proof? Was it even proof of anything, it just had the same design? Would she leave her fingerprints on it? The thought startled her. The last thing she wanted to do was to implicate herself. Instead she pulled out her cell phone to take a picture of the glass. When the bright flash flickered through the room her heart dropped. She'd forgotten the flash was on. Outside in the hall she heard footsteps. Within seconds she would be caught.

How could she explain breaking into the mayor's office? Even if his glass had the same design as the one that someone laced with poison, it didn't prove that he was the killer. She however would be very guilty of breaking and entering. Her chest tightened when the door pushed open. There was nowhere to hide. A flashlight shined right into her eyes. Blinded, Ally couldn't even see who stood in front of her.

"Ally, did you find anything?"

Relief flooded her as she recognized her grandmother's voice.

"Mee-Maw, what are you doing here?"

"I couldn't let you do this alone, Ally."

"But if we get caught..."

"So, let's not. Did you find what you needed?"

"Yes, I think so. We should hurry." Ally guided her out of the office. She quickly locked the door and then returned the key to the bottom drawer. She guided her grandmother back down the hallway. They were almost to the elevator when a security guard entered the hall.

"Hey! Who's down there?"

"Hurry, get to the elevator." Ally herded her grandmother in front of her. "Don't look back, Mee-Maw, just get to the elevator."

"Hey!" The security guard shouted. "Stop

right there!"

Ally jammed her finger into the button to open the doors. As soon as they slid open she gave her grandmother a little shove through the doors.

"Ally, hurry up, come on." Charlotte turned around to face her. Ally pushed the button to close the doors. Before Charlotte could get them back open the elevator started going down. Ally spun around to face the security guard.

"I'm sorry, I'm so sorry."

"What are you doing here?" He glared at her.

She held her hands up in the air. "It's so embarrassing. Really. I was here for a meeting and I lost my ring."

"A ring?"

"It's a little loose on my finger."

"That's not an explanation."

"Look, the thing is, it's a special ring. My grandmother gave it to me. I knew if I didn't get it back she would be heartbroken. So, I just wanted to see if I could get it back."

"And there was some reason you couldn't come back in the morning and ask the receptionist?"

"I was just so embarrassed. I had this horrible argument with the mayor's wife, and I didn't think he would let me in his office after that, and I just really needed the ring."

"Well, I hope you needed it enough to spend some time in jail, because that's where you're headed."

"Really?" She frowned. "Isn't there anything that I can do? It's not like I caused any harm. I didn't even get my ring back."

"No harm?"

"Nothing, I swear. I didn't even get inside the office. Can't you consider letting it slide?"

"What's in it for me?" He put his hand on his hip and gazed at her.

"Chocolate."

"Chocolate?"

"I can provide you with a year's supply of

freshly made delicious chocolate candy."

"Oh, like they have at Charlotte's Chocolate Heaven?"

"Exactly like they have at Charlotte's Chocolate Heaven. I promise."

He sighed and scratched his head. "This is my job we're talking about."

"And the best chocolate in town, no matter where you work."

"You're sure you didn't cause me any trouble?"

"None at all."

"Okay." He nodded. "Get out of here before I change my mind."

She didn't hesitate. With a quick push of the button the elevator doors opened. Ally stepped inside and hit the button for the lobby. As the elevator descended she began to relax. She wasn't out of the building yet, but she was close. Only then did she realize just how close she had come to being arrested. Her chest tightened as the elevator rocked to a stop in the lobby. She left the building as quickly as she could. As she rushed to her car she spotted her grandmother beside it.

"Mee-Maw, what were you thinking?" Ally paused in front of her.

"I was thinking that I couldn't let my granddaughter take such a big risk without me by her side. Does that really surprise you, Ally?"

"No." She frowned. "But I wish that you hadn't done that. I handled things just fine."

"Let me remind you, young lady, I am still the experienced one here. I don't need anyone to tell me what to do, or to be overprotective."

"Like you are to me?" Ally smiled and shook her head. "I guess we can't help but look out for each other."

"There are worse things in the world, hm?" Charlotte raised an eyebrow. Ally met her eyes and sighed.

"I guess you're right."

"Ally, breaking into the mayor's office was

over the top. It was too much of a risk. I think you need to slow down and get a grip on what you're actually doing here, before it's too late."

"Mee-Maw, I don't have time for a lecture. We need to get out of here before the security guard changes his mind."

"I'll meet you at the cottage."

"Really, it's late, you should go home."

"No, I'll meet you at the cottage." As Charlotte walked away Ally held her breath for a moment. It was fairly clear that her grandmother was upset. But so was she. In fact, she was a bit scared. She tried to steady her breath to remain calm. She needed to concentrate on the road. When she reached the cottage, her grandmother pulled in right behind her. Before she could get to the door Charlotte called out to her.

"Ally wait. If you go inside you're going to get distracted by the animals."

"You're right." Ally leaned back against the door of her car. "We can talk here."

"Do you think you were on camera?"

"I was careful to keep my head down. I know that much at least. Even if they think to look at the cameras, which they shouldn't have a reason to unless the security guard doesn't want his chocolate, they shouldn't be able to see anything."

"Okay good." She fluttered her hand against her chest. "Well, what's done is done, so let's try to focus on the good that might have come out of it."

"I think some did."

"So, what did you find?"

"Look." Ally flipped to the photograph on her phone. The moment she saw the picture her heart dropped. The glass with the identical pattern was there, but so was a clear image of her reflection. "It's a water glass, but it has the same pattern as the champagne glass."

"That is the same pattern." Charlotte narrowed her eyes. "But we can't turn this into the police. If we do they'll know that you broke into the mayor's office. That would go very badly for you."

"I know." Ally groaned and struck her forehead with the heel of her palm. "How could I be so stupid?"

"You're not stupid, Ally. Things happen. The important thing is that we know the glass most likely came from the mayor's office."

"Or maybe the champagne glass is at home. If they're part of a set he might keep the other ones at his home."

"Maybe. But the question is, how did it get to the country club? Did he bring it? Did someone else plant it?"

"Good question." Ally turned towards the kitchen door. "But I think they're going to have to be addressed tomorrow. I am wiped out."

"I bet you are. The next time you think it's a good idea to fall on your sword, just remember, I am tough, Ally, and judges go easier on little old ladies."

Ally rolled her eyes. "Let me know when you find a little old lady, and I'll think about letting her take the rap."

"Okay, good point." Charlotte grinned. "I have to admit, working with you on this is pretty thrilling, but this tonight, it was over the top."

"I hear you, Mee-Maw. I really do."

"I hope so." Charlotte met her eyes. "Because there is no way you're going to get away with breaking into the mayor's home. Understand?"

Ally nodded a little. "Not tonight."

"Not ever." Charlotte pointed a finger towards her. "That is far too much of a risk."

Ally nodded again. "I'd better get inside. Do you want to spend the night?"

"No, I think it's best if I head home. With all of this adrenaline I might be up for a few more hours. Though, I'll try to get some sleep since the memorial is tomorrow."

"Oh, that's right." Ally shook her head. "I'd almost forgotten."

"It's important that we be there I think."

"I wouldn't miss it."

"I'll meet you in the morning and we can go together?"

"Yes." Ally met her eyes as a pang of guilt coursed through her. "I'm sorry if I've stirred things up."

"I understand why you did."

"I'm sorry I scared you, Mee-Maw. Really, I am." Ally wrapped her arms around her for a warm hug

"It's okay. I know just how brave you are. Let's just take the time to think things through a little more from now on." She kissed her cheek. "Get some rest, okay?"

"I will."

Chapter Twelve

As Ally disappeared through the door of the cottage Charlotte couldn't help but wonder if she'd sneak out in the middle of the night and try to break into the mayor's home. She trusted Ally without question, but she also knew how determined she was to find justice. The worry nagged her the entire drive home. By the time she settled in, she knew she had to make a choice. She pulled out her phone and skimmed through the contacts. Then she started to put her phone away, only to pull it back out again.

Charlotte passed the phone back and forth and wondered if she should dial the number. As a rule she had stayed out of Ally's big decisions in life. Even though she hadn't liked the man she'd chosen to marry, she kept that to herself. She knew what it was like to be a young woman striking out on her own, and there was no reason not to trust Ally's ability to make decisions for herself. Now, what she considered doing, seemed like a betrayal. However, there were some ways that she could not reach Ally. She would always see Charlotte more as a parent than a peer and as someone who gave advice more out of protectiveness than wisdom.

After the risk Ally took by breaking into the mayor's office, Charlotte was very concerned. What would Ally do next? The fact that she even mentioned breaking into the mayor's home made Charlotte very uncomfortable. It was one thing to take a few risks while investigating a crime it was quite another to end up in jail for a very long time because of it. Ally couldn't see past her need to find justice for Julia, to realize that she was risking too much. It was obvious to Charlotte that the conversation they had wasn't enough to convince Ally either.

Without many options left, Charlotte felt there was only one thing that she could do. She dialed the number and waited for the line to pick up. She paced back and forth with each ring that passed. Was it too late? Would he not pick up because it was her? At the last ring she almost hung up. She almost talked herself out of following through with the call. Before she could push the button, she heard his voice.

"Charlotte, is everything okay?"

"Luke, I'm so sorry to bother you."

"It's no bother, though I'm guessing if you're calling me, something must be up."

"It is, and it isn't. I guess you've heard about the murder?"

"I have, on the news. I thought Ally might call me about it but she hasn't. I have been flat out, but I was going to call Ally tonight to check if everything was okay with you two because I know you were at the cocktail party when the deputy mayor was poisoned."

"As always Ally is trying to figure out who did it. From what we've found the evidence points to Mayor Malcolm, which of course makes it a bit tricky especially seeing as it's such a high profile case."

"Wow, that's complicated. Who has been dealing with it from the Freely police department?"

"I've had contact with an Officer John Frank."

"Oh boy, he's a transfer. Very by the book. I wouldn't expect him to be very forthcoming with information."

"Yes, we've found that out." She cringed and gripped the phone a little tighter. "I wouldn't want you to be distracted, but the reason I'm calling is because I was hoping that you could talk to Ally for me."

"Okay," Luke said hesitantly. "What do you want me to talk to her about?"

"Well, we had a close encounter tonight." Charlotte paused. She knew that she was taking a risk by providing Luke with the information, but she trusted him and needed his help. "She broke into the mayor's office."

"What?" Luke's voice raised so high that Charlotte pulled the phone away from her ear. "I hope that you're joking." He sighed.

"No, I'm not. That's why I'm calling. I'm worried about the risks she's taking. I tried to talk to her about it, but she wouldn't listen. I think that she's determined to break into the mayor's home, and I'm afraid that she'll get arrested."

"If she gets arrested breaking into the mayor's home she could be looking at serious prison time. I'll call her right now."

"Wait, Luke?"

"Yes?"

"I really shouldn't have called you about this. It's just that I'm worried about her, and I think she might listen to you. So just keep in mind, she's doing this for the right reasons."

"Don't worry, Charlotte, I always keep that in mind. Ally has such a kind heart. Thank you for trusting me enough to call me."

"You're welcome. Good luck." She hung up the phone with a sense of anxiety still brewing inside. Did she make the right choice by calling him? All she knew for sure was that she wanted to keep Ally safe. She just hoped that she hadn't made a mistake and overstepped.

As Charlotte curled up in bed she thought about her life with Ally. As fiercely as she loved Ally's mother, her love for her granddaughter was just as strong. Without Ally's mother to guide her, that responsibility fell on Charlotte's shoulders, and she would never forgive herself if she failed at it. However, if calling Luke meant that Ally was safer in the long run, then it was worth it.

***

As soon as Ally walked in the door, she heard the high pitched squeals. That was a familiar sound to her, but this time it was a little different.

"Oh no, Arnold, what have you been up to?" As she took a step into the kitchen she realized immediately what the problem was. Pig feed crunched beneath her feet. She flicked the light on to discover that the entire kitchen floor was covered with it. The entire floor, except for the part that Arnold had his snout buried in.

"Arnold! No!" Ally sighed as she realized the amount of walks he was going to need. "I guess it's not really your fault, I'm the one who left the bag on the counter." She picked up the remains of the bag and what food was left inside. Then she looked from the pig to the counter. "Except, pigs can't reach that high." She huffed. "Peaches!" A blur of fur blew by the kitchen door. Ally couldn't help but laugh. Even though the kitchen was a mess, and Arnold's stomach looked rounder than ever, she couldn't be angry. She was late to feed them both, and Peaches had stepped in to save the day. She shooed Arnold away from the remaining food and set about sweeping it up. After she salvaged what she could, she turned her attention to Peaches. The cat was probably famished. She set out a larger bowl than normal. As soon as the bowl hit the floor Peaches bolted into the kitchen.

"Oh, not too scared to get your dinner, hm?" She smiled and reached down to stroke along the cat's back. "Thanks for taking care of Arnold for me, Peaches. I'm sorry that I was so late. I got a little lost in looking into this murder." She sighed and went to look for Arnold's leash. When she clipped it onto his collar he waddled his way towards the door.

Outside in the crisp air Ally was reminded of the break-in. It was nice to breathe fresh air. If the guard didn't fall for her charm and her chocolate, she might be stuck in a cell right that second. The thought made her shiver despite it not being very cold outside. She closed her eyes for a moment while Arnold sniffed a tree and thought about what she could have done differently. She had the picture, sure, but what good would that do? As Mee-Maw pointed out all it really was to the police at the moment, was evidence of her breaking into a government office. She didn't want to risk turning it over, especially with Luke away. As if he sensed her thoughts, her phone rang.

She looked at the phone and saw it was Luke. She thought about not answering.

The issue was not that she didn't want to talk to him. The issue was that she would likely say too much. Luke had a way of drawing the truth out of her that she couldn't quite understand. Just before it went to voicemail she picked up.

"Hi Luke!" Ally answered cheerfully.

"Ally." His tone was hard.

"Is something wrong?"

"That's what I'm trying to figure out. I just had an interesting conversation with your grandmother."

Ally's heart sunk. A sharp anger rose in its place as she took a long slow breath. "Oh, she's just overreacting."

"Is she? Maybe you can let me know which thing she told me was untrue. Was it the thing about you breaking into the mayor's office? Or was it the thing about you being determined to break into his home?"

Ally looked up at the stars that littered the sky. Even at a distance Luke had a way of cutting right through all of her defenses.

"It's all for the sake of solving a murder, Luke.

I'm being careful."

"Ally, I can understand why you want to solve it, but you need to realize that the police are going to be all over this. They're not going to let this go easily."

"Maybe not, but I have to find out the truth. One minute she was smiling, the next..."

"Ally, I do understand why you want to find her murderer, but I also know that you are being reckless. Your grandmother is worried about you, worried enough to call me, so that tells me she's not getting through to you and Charlotte isn't exactly averse to taking risks."

"All the evidence is pointing to Mayor Malcolm, I'm not sure that the police are going to be willing to investigate him properly."

"Don't sell them short. Remember, people don't join the police force to turn a blind eye to murder."

"I know, I know." She sighed. "But I can't shake this feeling that everything is going to be swept under the rug."

"It won't be, you have to have some faith."

"Luke, I'm close to figuring this out. I just want to get to the bottom of this. I'll be careful."

"What can I say that will make you realize just how much danger you're putting yourself in? Not only is the mayor a powerful and influential person, he also may not be the killer. By investigating you may be exposing yourself to the killer."

"I know, I know. I've thought all of that through, Luke, but it doesn't change anything. Someone has to get to the bottom of this, and right now that someone has to be me."

"Please, just take a minute and think about this, Ally. Even if you do find the evidence that you need, it'll be tainted. A judge has to order a search warrant and..."

"Okay, okay, I hear you," Ally said.

"Do you?"

"Yes, I won't break into the mayor's home."

"Good. I'll look into it when I get back. But hopefully it will be solved before then. Just be patient."

"What if someone else gets killed?"

"I'm sure they won't, but that's not your problem. The police will get to the bottom of this. Just slow down, and think about what you're doing."

"I can't believe Mee-Maw called you."

"She's worried, and obviously didn't think that you were going to listen to her. Please just relax and leave this to the police."

"All right." Ally nodded and glanced back up at the sky. "I will."

"Good. I'm sure this will be solved in no time."

As soon as the line disconnected Ally felt her heart slow down. So Luke knew. What difference did that make? She thought about being angry with her grandmother, but she couldn't be. Luke was right. She had only called him out of concern. Still, it did make her a little uneasy that the two of them were talking behind her back, but also happy that they got along so well. Now that breaking into the mayor's home was off the table, she had to come up with a new plan.

Chapter Thirteen

When Ally returned to the house she settled Arnold into his bed which she had put at the foot of her bed. Then she took a quick shower to calm her nerves. No matter what she did she knew that she was going to be faced with some hard choices. Not the least of which was whether to simply leave the case in the hands of the police. Maybe if Luke was there she would be more inclined to do just that, but probably not.

Once she was in her pajamas she stretched out on her bed and curled a pillow under her head. Peaches jumped up onto the bed beside her. Her purr soothed Ally's nerves more than the shower did. She stroked her hand through the cat's silky fur and began to relax. Ally closed her eyes and tried to sleep, but the ability to do so was washed away by the memory of Luke's voice. She appreciated that he cared enough to call, but it bothered her that he thought she couldn't make a wise decision. She hadn't broken into the mayor's home yet. That had to count for something. She flipped over in her bed and sighed. Peaches meowed and paced back and forth across her back. Ally relaxed a little.

"Thanks Peaches. I needed a kitty massage." She buried her face in her pillow and tried to force any chaotic thoughts out of her mind. Instead, she envisioned confronting the mayor. What could the consequences of that be? He might have connections in Blue River and be able to get the license for the shop rescinded, maybe he could even influence the health inspector if he wanted to. She tightened her eyes as she wondered if she'd made an enemy out of the wrong man. If she had, there wasn't much chance of repairing that relationship. Not that she would want to if what she suspected was true. Was he Julia's killer?

Her mind retreated to the party, to the way that Julia coughed. It was so out of the blue. Ally thought perhaps she still had a bit of food in her mouth when she began the speech. She had some water. Her husband had handed it to her. Then

Mayor Malcolm gave her his glass of champagne. Who would be stupid enough to openly hand someone a poisoned glass of champagne in front of a room full of people? Certainly not the mayor. Maybe he was framed. Maybe he orchestrated the whole thing. Maybe he made it his own glass to create a sense of disbelief. She tossed and turned again. She stretched her body as far as it could go. Peaches stretched out beside her and offered a sleepy yawn.

"I know, I know. I'm keeping you awake." Ally sighed and pet the cat as her thoughts calmed. Finally, she closed her eyes. As she drifted off to sleep her mind wandered to the thought of Luke returning home and the subtle pang of just how much she missed him.

She was jolted awake hours later by her alarm. Dazed, she reached for her clock and almost knocked it off the table. All at once it struck her that it was the day of the memorial. The day that Julia would be buried in a small ceremony with her family and close friends, while simultaneously being remembered at a public memorial in the middle of town. It was a day to honor her memory.

Ally quickly jumped into the shower to wake herself up. She dressed and then headed for the kitchen. As the coffee brewed she tried to focus on the good that could come from the day. A woman who had a great influence on the town would be honored by those that loved her. Maybe a truth would be revealed at some point. Maybe Ally would get a step closer to figuring out what really happened. But before any of that could happen, she had to have a conversation with her grandmother. She prepared breakfast for Arnold and Peaches. The scream of the teapot drowned out the meows and squeals. Ally moved the teapot off the burner in time to hear a knock on the door.

"Come on in, Mee-Maw!" Ally poured a cup of tea and carried it to the table. Arnold squealed with joy as Charlotte made her way into the kitchen. Peaches even tore herself away from her food to offer Charlotte a warm greeting. She wound her way around Charlotte's legs and purred. Charlotte reached down and pet the cat. Then she crouched down and made kissing noises at Arnold. Arnold slowly spun around in happy circles.

"Good morning." Charlotte smiled at Ally. "Thank you for the tea." She sat down at the table, but didn't touch the hot drink. She also avoided her granddaughter's gaze.

Ally leaned back against the counter and raised an eyebrow as she folded her arms across her stomach. "We need to talk, Mee-Maw."

"Oh? About the murder?"

"Not exactly." Ally sat down across from her with her own cup of tea. "How could you call Luke?"

Charlotte frowned and offered a quick glance up at her. "I'm sorry, Ally, I didn't know what else to do. You weren't listening to me, and I was worried."

"Mee-Maw, I can handle myself. You know

me well enough to know that."

"Normally, yes I would agree. But you're making choices that concern me."

"I'm making choices that are getting us information about solving a murder."

"Like you did with that guard last night? What if he didn't like chocolate? I'd be at the police station right now trying to bail you out."

"I know." Ally looked down into her own cup of tea. "I was more than a little reckless. I'm sorry about that."

"You are?" Charlotte looked up at her. "I didn't expect that reaction."

"I just wanted to find out the truth so badly. In the end I put us both in a very risky position. At the time it seemed like a good idea. Looking back, I'm just relieved that nothing bad happened."

"I guess that Luke got through to you."

"No, Mee-Maw, you did. What you said last night sank in. Plus, the fact that you would go to Luke even though you knew it would upset me, shows me just how worried you are. I wish I hadn't made you that worried."

"It's okay, sweetheart. All that matters is that you stay safe. That's all I want for you."

"I know that, I just don't know how I can let this go. If the mayor is the murderer he shouldn't get away with it just because he is powerful and people are afraid of him."

"No, he shouldn't, but it's been happening for generations, Ally. One thing about the world is that it changes very, very, slowly. You can't fight something that is so ingrained."

"Maybe. Or maybe there's another way to come at it."

"What are you thinking?"

"I'm not sure yet. Maybe there's something we're missing here. I can tell you that I will be more careful though."

"So, you're not going to break into the mayor's home?"

"No, I'm not." She smiled. "That is too big of

a risk. There are other ways to get to the bottom of things."

"Ally, I'm sorry that I called Luke behind your back, I hope you understand I only did it out of love."

"Don't be sorry, Mee-Maw, it's good to know that you have my back even when I don't know I need it. Bonus, I got to have a conversation with Luke. I just hope I can find out who the murderer is."

"Oh you can, sweetheart. I have no doubt in my mind."

Ally reached across the table and gave her hand a light squeeze. "Together we can, Mee-Maw."

"I believe that, Ally. But remember, today is not about the investigation. It's about honoring the life that was lost."

"I hope that we find out something about her murder though."

"Just be patient. The truth has a way of always

coming out. I was thinking since parking is going to be crazy in the Freely town center, why don't we just walk there?"

"Good idea." Ally nodded. Freely was in walking distance even though it was a bit of a hike. "I could use a nice walk. I have a couple of muffins from the shop, would you like one?"

"Sure."

Ally got two muffins and handed her grandmother one. When she put it down in front of her, Charlotte looked up and met her eyes.

"Are you sure that you're not mad at me?"

"I'm honestly not, Mee-Maw." Ally sat back down and took a bite of her muffin. "Actually, I'm impressed that you trusted Luke enough to go to him. I guess that's an official seal of approval."

"He does seem to be a good man." Charlotte took a bite of her muffin and chewed it thoughtfully. "He certainly cares about you."

"How lucky am I?" Ally grinned. She stood up to clear the dishes and nearly tripped over a pig.

The plates flew out of her hand as she caught herself on the edge of the counter. Arnold squealed as the plates shattered when they struck the sink.

"Oh no." Charlotte jumped up. "Are you okay, Ally?"

"I'm okay." Ally laughed. "I guess I shouldn't call myself lucky."

"Or maybe this pig needs to learn some manners." Charlotte put her hands on her hips and looked down at Arnold. "I don't know how many times I've had to tell you this, Arnold. You are a pig, not a cat."

Arnold snorted and looked from Charlotte to Ally.

"Aw, he's okay." Ally patted his back. "He just wants to go for a walk. Let me take him for a quick stroll then we'll head out."

"Okay." Charlotte stepped up to the sink. "I'll take care of these plates for you."

"Thanks." Ally snapped on Arnold's leash and

led him outside. Not far from the cottage she noticed most of her neighbors getting into cars and driving off towards Freely. There was no doubt in her mind that it would be a very crowded event. Arnold seemed to sense this, too. He was distracted by every car that pulled out of the driveway. Ally glanced at her watch. It was later than she had planned to leave.

"Let's go, Arnold, I don't want to be late."

Ally turned back towards the cottage with Arnold. When she did she caught a glimpse of what she thought was a camera flash just beyond the driveway behind a group of trees. Her heart stopped for a second. Did she see what she thought she saw? Was it just the headlights of a car pulling out of a driveway? Or maybe a floodlight left on and just switched off? Her heart began to pound. She held tight to Arnold's leash and made her way towards the trees. By the time she reached them whoever might have been there before was gone. She didn't see any evidence that anyone had been there. Ally frowned and hurried

Arnold back inside. Charlotte met her at the door.

"We have to get going if we want to walk."

"Yes, I know." Ally grabbed her purse and made sure that Arnold had some water. Then they rushed out the door together.

"Is something wrong?" Charlotte took a moment to look at her.

"Maybe." Ally frowned. "I don't know. I thought I saw someone take a picture of me."

"Hm. What made you think that?"

"I saw the flash through the trees over there." She pointed at the clump of trees near the house.

"Are you sure that someone was there?"

"I'm really not. I'm starting to think that I'm just getting a little paranoid."

"It's all right, this kind of situation will do that to you. Let's not worry about it now. I want to try to focus on Julia."

Ally slipped her hand into her grandmother's. "You're right, today isn't about that. Today is about honoring Julia. Although I didn't know her, I feel like I know her a little better now. I feel like she would have been at the front of this group to honor anyone else."

"She would have been." Charlotte smiled fondly. "She was the type of woman that took up for any cause that she thought had value. She didn't just stand behind one belief, she stood behind anyone who needed help. That's why she was so supportive of the initiative to have all services provided by local businesses. She agreed with the mayor, that if people worked where they lived, then the pride within the city would only go up. She loved Freely. Many politicians don't love the town they govern the way she did. She was born in Blue River you know, but she had spent most of her life in Freely."

"No, I didn't know that. I'm surprised that I didn't know her."

"You two missed each other. Her family moved to Freely when she was very young, before you were born. I'm sure you saw her here and there."

Once they reached Freely they joined the flood of people that headed towards the main square either on foot or in their cars.

"I guess that there are many people that admired her." Ally nodded her head towards the crowd that gathered around the main square. It was at least ten people deep and spanned most of the main street. Ally hoped that like her they were gathered there to celebrate a life well lived.

"Yes. It's okay, Ally." Charlotte let go of her hand and wrapped her arm around her shoulders. "Justice will come soon enough."

Chapter Fourteen

Once Ally and Charlotte were in the main square Ally searched through the crowd of faces. Maybe the murderer was there. The main person she searched for was Mayor Malcolm. But she knew he wouldn't be there. He would be at the actual funeral. His presence there would have been expected. Still she looked for him, just in case. A man stood behind a microphone at the front of the crowd.

"That's Julia's replacement. Ted Housers. He seems like a pretty nice guy. It's a bit bold of him to take the lead at the memorial though," Charlotte said.

"Maybe not." Ally sighed. "Who else would?"

"Good point." Charlotte stood close to her.

"I think he was at the cocktail party."

"He was. He was seated at the table next to the main table."

"I think he came to the catering table to get a

tart."

"That's right." Charlotte nodded. "Maybe we can get a little further up. It's going to be hard to hear him even with the microphone."

"You go ahead. I want to stand back here and keep an eye on the whole crowd."

"Okay. Text me if you need me." Charlotte made her way through the crowd of people towards the front. Ally hung back and surveyed everyone around her. There weren't too many faces that she didn't have at least some familiarity with. Though most of the news crews were at the funeral, she noticed a few reporters. Then she saw him, hiding behind his camera, which was pointed right at her. She took a slight step back as she recognized Ralph. He noticed her noticing him and began to walk towards her. Her heart began to race. Was he the one hiding in the trees? Did he have reason to follow her?

"I thought that was you." He let his camera fall against his chest. "Did you find out anything new about the murder?"

"A bit." She nodded and avoided looking at him.

"I hope the pictures helped somehow."

"They did. But not enough. Not yet anyway." Ally stole a glance at him.

"Do you have a main suspect?"

"Why were you following me?" Ally asked.

He lowered his eyes and fiddled with his camera. "I thought maybe you had seen me."

"Well I did. Why were you following me?" She repeated.

"I was on my way to the memorial, and I saw you with the pig. It just seemed like a great photograph. So I parked and took the shot. I didn't think you'd let me if I asked."

"Why would I?" She crossed her arms. "You have no reason to take pictures of me."

"I get inspired by certain things, Ally. A pretty woman like you, taking comfort in a pot-bellied pig, you have to admit, that's a good photo."

"It's not right to snap pictures of people without permission."

"That's what I've based most of my career on. Do you want to see the picture?" He picked up his camera. Ally frowned.

"I guess."

He smiled and displayed the digital screen to her. "See?"

Ally stared at the photograph of her and Arnold together. She wanted to be angry, but the truth was, the picture was perfect. "Can you give me a copy?"

"I knew you would like it."

"Still, it's not right to do what you did."

"Okay, okay. I'm sorry. Now, can you tell me what you found out about Julia's murder?"

"Not much," Ally said. She didn't know if she could trust him with any information and she didn't want to risk it. She tried to change the subject. "Aren't you afraid that people will get angry with you for taking photos of them?"

"I'm not afraid." He grinned. "You should see the places I've been with this camera. Besides, I have my ways of protecting myself."

"How?" Ally swept her gaze over his wiry frame with disbelief.

"Easy now." He chuckled. "No, it's not with brute force. Let's just say, I make it my business to have a little something on everyone who could do me harm."

"Like blackmail?"

"It's not blackmail unless you use it." He quirked an eyebrow. "I've never had a reason to use any of it."

"What about me?" She stared into his eyes. "Do you have anything on me?"

"I did." He smirked. "But, I think it's useless now."

"What do you mean?"

"I caught a snap of you and your officer boyfriend in an affectionate moment. I thought it would be good to use in case there was ever an issue with me getting information from the detective. But, since you two aren't exactly hiding your affection, I guess it's not going to do much for me now."

Ally rolled her eyes. "I guess it was worth invading my privacy for that silly photograph."

"The thing that people don't realize, is that I don't invade anything. I don't secretly follow people around to find dirt on them. People are so numb to the fact that they are constantly surrounded by others, that they air their dirty laundry out in public. If I happen to catch it, that's merely observation, not invasion."

Ally shrugged. "You can call it what you want, but you are using photography as a weapon."

"Am I now?" He stared at her with wide eyes. "I can see that your disdain for me is clear."

"It's not you." She sighed. "I'm just frustrated with trying to find out who killed Julia. It seems to me that people in power get away with way too much."

"Not when it comes to this camera." He tapped the top of it. "Actually, that's the real reason I came over here."

"What do you mean?" Ally turned to look at him again.

"I have something that I thought might be helpful."

"You do? What is it?"

"It's not so much what it is, but who it is. I have some interesting pictures of the mayor and Julia."

"Do you have them with you?"

"No, of course not. I have them at home. I'm not going to risk walking around with something like that. I can show them to you if you want."

Ally chewed on her bottom lip for a moment. She wasn't sure whether to trust him. However, the temptation of the photographs was too much to ignore.

"After the memorial."

"Okay, I'll find you." He smirked and tilted his

head to the side. "You're going to like what I found, trust me." Then he turned and walked back into the crowd. Ally wondered what the pictures were of. She hoped they were something she could use to further the case and not just smut. She had believed that the rumors about Julia and Mayor Malcolm, were just that, rumors, but maybe she was wrong. As the memorial came to a close Ally looked through the crowd for her grandmother. She spotted her surrounded by a few other business owners. Charlotte broke away from them when she spotted Ally.

"Are you holding up okay?" She gave Ally's shoulder a squeeze.

"It was a nice memorial."

"Yes, I thought so, too. Ted gave a good speech. He's also hosting the dinner and drinks they're having at the restaurant down the street. Should we head over now?"

"I have to meet someone. Then I'll be back for the dinner."

"Ally, who are you meeting?" Charlotte

searched her eyes for an answer.

"Not now, Mee-Maw." She looked around at the people close by to indicate to her grandmother that she didn't want it to be overheard. "I will tell you later I promise."

"Ally, you're not doing anything rash are you?"

"I'm not, I promise."

"Remember to be careful."

"I will." As Ally started to walk away her grandmother followed her. Once they were away from the crowd she grabbed Ally's arm to stop her.

"You're not thinking of breaking into the mayor's home while he's at the funeral, are you?"

Ally raised her eyebrows. "No I wasn't, but now that you mention it, that's a pretty great idea."

"Ally!"

Ally laughed and shook her head. "I promise, I'm not breaking in anywhere. I've been invited. I am just going to look at some photos that the photographer took. Apparently he has some photos that might be interesting."

"Okay, be careful."

Ally turned and walked away from the main square. Not far from the street she saw another gathering. She spotted Ralph in the parking lot. He had a group of people around him as he snapped pictures. Ally walked up to the edge of the group and watched as Ralph continued to snap away.

Ally noticed that one of the men in the group was Ted Housers, the new deputy mayor of Freely. Her heart skipped a beat as it occurred to her that Ted profited quite a bit from Julia's death. He now had a brand new title, and more than likely a huge increase in pay. Would that be reason enough for him to poison her or the mayor? She narrowed her eyes. He was at the next table over, he could have poisoned the mayor's glass. He could probably access poison with his political reach. Just as her mind began to churn with the possibility of him being the killer, Ralph lowered the camera.

"Hi there, Ally." He waved to her. Ted Housers turned to look. When he saw Ally he smiled. Ally looked into his eyes and noted that he seemed quite genuine. But that didn't mean he was. "Just taking the time to take some pictures for the new deputy mayor."

"Please, this isn't the day to call me that." Ted waved his hand at Ralph. "I want to honor Julia today, not do anything to taint her memory. She was my inspiration, and I only hope that I can half fill the shoes she left behind."

Ally's heart softened a little at his words. But did he mean them?

"Excuse us." Ralph gestured to Ally who followed him towards the edge of the lot. "So, I guess you want to see what I've got?"

"I do."

"It's going to cost you."

"Seriously? You're going to make me pay?"

"No, I just want a favor."

"A favor? Chocolate?"

"No, I'm allergic, remember?"

"Oh yes. Then what?"

"I want a chance to have dinner with you."

"I thought you knew that Luke and I are kind of..."

"Kind of." He tilted his head towards her. "That's the point isn't it? Anyway, it will just be a dinner between friends."

"Why?" Ally frowned.

"What do you mean, why?" He stared back at her.

"Why would you want to have dinner with me?"

"I thought it would be nice to have dinner so I can get to know you better. Unless you'd consent to a photo shoot instead?"

"Absolutely not." She shook her head. With her hands shoved in her pockets she considered his offer. She did want to see the pictures, however a dinner out with another man might not go over well with Luke. Still, he said it was just as friends. Ally looked into his eyes. "Just as friends?"

"I'll be on my best behavior. Unless, you don't want me to be." He offered a smile.

"No, I want you to be. Okay fine. Can we go and see those pictures now?"

"Right this way." He gestured to a car not far from him.

"I'll meet you there."

"In what?" He looked around. Ally remembered that she had left her car at the cottage and walked into Freely with her grandmother. It would take far too long to walk back, get her car, and then drive to his house. She sighed and nodded.

"All right, I'll ride with you."

"Just relax. Not every photographer is a secret psycho you know."

"Oh, I don't think everyone is. But I do wonder about you." Ally smiled.

"Rude!" Ralph laughed and shook his head. "I

might not enjoy dinner with you after all."

"You didn't say that you had to enjoy it."

"Good point." He opened the car door for her. "Get in."

Against her better judgment she sat down in the passenger seat of the car. He gunned the engine and the car roared off down the road. Ally glanced out the window at the disappearing crowd behind her and wondered if she'd made a grave mistake.

Chapter Fifteen

Ralph switched on the radio and turned up the volume. As the rock music blasted out of the speakers Ally's heart began to pound along with the beat. She glanced over at Ralph. He looked calm, and fairly normal. But what sense did it make for her to get in a car with someone she barely knew? Someone who just that morning took secret pictures of her? He could be driving her anywhere.

"What are the pictures of, Ralph?"

"You'll find out when we get there." Ralph raised his voice to be heard over the music. When he looked over at her his eyes were stern. Ally stared back at him, then pointed her finger towards the road.

"Stay focused."

"Okay, okay." He nodded and sped up even more. Ally grabbed the door handle and closed her eyes. At the very least if he kept driving the way he was then they would likely be pulled over. Before that could happen he came to a sharp stop. "My house!" Ralph said barely above a whisper.

Ally opened her eyes to see what remained of Ralph's house. The roof was charred. The walls slumped as if they might collapse at any moment.

"What?" Ralph stuttered out the word. He didn't say another word. He just repeated the same one. When he opened the car door the car continued to roll. He put the car into park, then jumped out. Ally stepped out of the passenger side and stared at the house as well. Curls of smoke still rose from the structure. A fireman stood near the driveway of the house. Ralph walked towards him, though his eyes didn't leave the house.

"Sir? You can't go in there." The fireman walked towards him.

"What?" Ralph finally looked at him. Ally stepped up beside him.

"What happened?" She asked what Ralph couldn't manage to spit out.

"A fire," the fireman said.

Ally had to resist the desire to roll her eyes. "I see that. But how? When did it start?"

"We were called when it was already engulfed. Unfortunately, with everyone being in town for the memorial I guess the fire wasn't noticed very fast. We tried to save the house, but it was too far gone when we arrived."

"This is impossible." Ralph ran his hand back through his hair. "All of my pictures are gone. My cameras. Everything was in there."

"Try to calm down, Sir. Some things may be salvageable."

"But how did it happen?" Ally narrowed her eyes.

"Our best guess at this point was a chemical fire from the chemicals in the dark room."

"No, absolutely not. That is not what happened. I am very careful with all of my chemicals. I always double-check to make sure that everything is off and unplugged. My entire life is in that house. I am always careful."

"Something started the fire. At this point we don't know what that was. We will conduct a full investigation. I hope that you have insurance."

"I do. But that's not going to get the pictures back. I have backups of some, but nothing replaces the originals. What am I going to do?"

"Just take a deep breath. You have to let them do their investigation, then they will get to the bottom of it," Ally said.

"Someone did this." Ralph thrust his fist through the air. "I know it!"

"Ralph, is there anyone you can call? Anyone that you can stay with?" Ally tried to get his attention with a light touch on his shoulder. He whipped around so fast that she stumbled back.

"No! I don't want to stay with anyone. I want my house back!" He groaned. "I knew it. I knew this would happen if I wasn't careful. Who did you tell about the pictures of the party that I showed to you?"

Ally took another step back. "I didn't tell anyone."

"Don't lie to me!" He pointed a finger so close to her face that she could have bitten it. "You were the only one that I showed the pictures to. Someone must know what was in those pictures, otherwise this wouldn't have happened. There is no other reason for someone to want to burn down my place."

"I just told my grandmother that's it. She wouldn't have told anyone." Ally stared into his eyes. "Just relax, Ralph, you've got to get a hold of yourself. Something terrible has happened, but at least no one was hurt."

"No one was hurt?" His eyes filled with tears. "Do you know what I had inside of that house? Years worth of work! Years!" He reached up and pulled at his own hair. "All nothing but ash now!"

Startled by the passionate tone of his voice, Ally again tried to comfort him with a light touch to his shoulder.

"It's devastating, you're right. Why don't you

come back to my place, you can calm down a little, and we'll talk about the next step."

"No." He narrowed his eyes. "You've done enough." He started to turn away from her, but Ally tugged at his wrist.

"Wait, Ralph! What about the pictures that you were going to show me?"

He laughed and shook his head. "The pictures. That's all you care about. Fine. They were photographs of Mayor Malcolm and a female politician."

"Julia?"

"No, but she was also there. I have a series of pictures. The mayor and this politician, Sue Wardie, at a fancy restaurant. Then in comes Julia, who ends up throwing the mayor's glass of champagne into his face. I have it all on camera."

"Was she jealous?"

"Not according to the other people that were in the restaurant that night. Julia apparently accused him of going behind her back trying to

181

make a political deal with Sue that Julia didn't want to go ahead. I've heard all of the rumors that people spread about the mayor and Julia, but I don't believe any of it. If anything had happened between them I would have found some indication of their affair over the years, but I haven't. I doubt she was having an affair with him."

"That wasn't what I expected."

"I didn't think it would be."

"Do you think Sue Wardie could have held a grudge against Julia and killed her?"

"No, she moved from Freely a couple of months ago so she was no longer interested in the Freely government."

"Okay. I guess that rules her out," Ally said thoughtfully.

"Don't miss out on the key detail, Ally."

Ally frowned. "What's that?"

He rolled his eyes. "I'll spell it out for you. Julia humiliated the mayor by throwing the champagne in his face. Then she died from a poisoned glass of champagne."

"Oh!" Ally's eyes widened. "I see it now."

"I should hope so." He stared hard at her. "I have to go figure out what I can save from my house. I hope you can get your own ride home."

"I can." Ally bit into her bottom lip. "But are you sure that you're going to be okay?"

"You have your information, there's no need to pretend to care anymore." He waved his hand. "Scurry along."

Ally considered an attempt at trying to offer to help him again. But she recalled the secret pictures, and his insistence on having dinner with her. It was probably best to let things end as they were. Without another word she turned and walked away from the smoldering house. A sense of anxiety ruffled her nerves as she thought about what kind of person would just burn down a house. Ally pulled out her cell phone as she walked back towards the end of the road. She dialed her grandmother's number and waited for her to answer. After the third ring she did.

"Ally, are you okay?"

"Yes, I am. I'm sorry to pull you away, Mee-Maw, but I need a ride. I know that we walked into Freely, is there any way that you could send someone out to get me?"

"Actually, I went back to the cottage. It was getting a little crazy in Freely. Where are you? I'll come pick you up right now."

Ally gave her the address and a condensed explanation of why she needed a lift. She decided to save the bit about the burnt down house until her grandmother arrived. As she waited for her, Ally paced back and forth. She mulled through all of the possibilities of what might have happened to Ralph's house. There was no question that the timing seemed rather odd. Maybe the mayor hired someone to torch it. Or maybe it was one of the many people that Ralph claimed to have blackmail information on. Someone might have been tired of the weight that Ralph had hanging over their head. Whoever did it might be ruthless, desperate, and not likely to stop there.

Chapter Sixteen

Charlotte pulled to a stop beside Ally, but her gaze focused on the remains of the house down the street.

"Ally? Did you burn a house down?"

Ally couldn't help but laugh a little as she got into the car. "No, it wasn't me. It's the photographer's house. I think someone did it on purpose."

"Who?" Charlotte raised an eyebrow. "The mayor?"

"I'm not sure. Did you notice if Ted Housers seemed eager to take Julia's position?"

"No, not really. Do you think so?"

"I don't know. He certainly is at a higher pay grade now."

"True." Charlotte drove back towards town. They had to park a few blocks away from the main square and walk to the restaurant.

People were already leaving the restaurant when they arrived. Ally noticed that there were extra chairs pulled up to several tables, so she presumed there had been a large attendance. Near the front of the restaurant Ted Housers shook hands and smiled sadly at everyone who passed him. Ally studied him from a distance as Charlotte found them a place to sit.

He looked the part, that was for sure. A three-piece suit, carefully combed hair, eager eyes that became sad at the exact moment someone looked at him. There were things about him that left her uneasy, but she couldn't place exactly what they were. He had to have worked closely with Julia and might know something that would help solve the murder. She waited until most people walked away from him, then approached. As she neared him he smiled in recognition.

"Good to see you again."

"You, too." Ally smiled. "I guess that you will be taking on a lot of new responsibilities."

"Yes, but I'm ready for it."

"Are you?" Ally raised an eyebrow. Before she could say another word the door to the restaurant burst open. Julia's husband burst inside, followed by Mayor Malcolm.

"How dare you?" He roared at Ted. Ted took a few steps back. Somehow Ally found herself between the two men, with Julia's husband's fury right in front of her.

"I know you're upset, but you need to think about what you're doing here," Mayor Malcolm said as he grabbed his arms and pulled him back a few steps. "Stop this now. Not like this. Look how many people are here."

"I don't care!" He squirmed out of Mayor Malcolm's grasp. "I don't care who knows anymore. Our entire marriage was a lie, she knew it, I knew it, but to have you host a dinner in her honor? Are you trying to rub my face in it?"

"What do you care?" Ted shouted back. Ally turned to face him and put a hand up to stop him from moving forward.

"I think you both need to calm down."

"No! If he wants to be honest, then let's be honest." Ted looked in Julia's husband's eyes and lowered his voice so only the people close to him could hear him. "I was the one that she loved, not you."

"You should have left her alone and she would have been fine!" Julia's husband said.

"That's enough!" Mayor Malcolm pushed Ally aside and put a hand on each of their chests. "Julia deserved better than this. Drop it, both of you, or I'll have you behind bars."

Ally stared at the three men entangled in a war over Julia. It occurred to her that she might have seemed like a very calm person on the surface, but it appeared that underneath she dealt with quite a bit of drama.

"Fine!" Her husband pulled away from the mayor and stormed towards the door of the restaurant. "What does it matter now? She's dead anyway." He slammed the door shut behind him. The restaurant erupted in whispers and the movement of chairs. Ally looked back at Ted who glared at Mayor Malcolm.

"You couldn't stop him?"

"He lost his wife, Ted."

"She should have been my wife." Ted hissed those words. "Don't I have a right to grieve?"

Mayor Malcolm held up his hands and shook his head. "We just have to find a way to get through this. We all lost her, Ted. We all did."

Something in Mayor Malcolm's voice made Ally's heart drop. It was genuine grief. Did he regret killing Julia? Or was he not involved at all? Ally joined Charlotte at a crowded table.

"How did you get in the middle of that?"

"I don't know exactly." Ally frowned as she looked at her grandmother. "I guess she really was well loved."

"What were they arguing about?" Charlotte asked. "I only caught snippets of their conversation."

"I'll fill you in in private."

"It's too tense in here for me. Do you want to stay?"

"No, let's get out of here. I think I've seen enough."

***

After Ally dropped Charlotte off at Freely Lakes and returned to the cottage she spent some time researching Ted Housers. Everything about him was squeaky clean. She did notice that he was married and she wondered how he got away with having an affair with Julia and not a trace of it was found in the newspapers or gossip pages. Maybe they were just very careful.

After taking a break for dinner she noticed that the local website was buzzing with news about Ralph's house. From the comments she had read it was clear that the house was a total loss, and also that Ralph was not going to get a lot of sympathy from the locals. After a few moments of consideration she dialed Ralph's number.

"What do you want?"

"I just wanted to check on you."

"Really?

"Yes, Ralph. I'm really sorry about your house."

"Don't be. I'll get a new one."

"Then I'm sorry about the drama."

"Why are you really calling me, Ally?"

"To see if you're okay and to check if you know that Julia and Ted Housers were in a relationship."

"Yes."

"Then why didn't you tell me?"

"I wasn't aware that I was required to tell you everything I know."

"Don't you think that Ted could be a suspect?"

"No." He cleared his throat. "I don't think that at all."

"Why not?"

"Listen. I did stumble upon their affair. Honestly, it restored my faith in romance. It was so obvious that they were so in love, I just couldn't reveal it."

"That's very thoughtful of you."

"I am more than just some guy hiding behind trees you know."

"Okay. Thanks again for your help, Ralph."

"Sure. If you need anything, just let me know." He hung up. Ally wasn't sure what to make of his final offer. He offered to help if she needed him. Maybe he wasn't as bad as she originally thought. She went to bed that night with a lot of different emotions weighing on her mind.

Chapter Seventeen

Ally woke up late the next morning. After the strange night she had, her mind was still awash with memories of the burned-out house and Ralph's revelation about what the pictures contained. Not to mention the affair between Ted and Julia. She rose to her feet and made her way to the kitchen in response to Peaches' loud demands for attention. She grabbed the can of cat food and started to prepare a bowl for Peaches. Before she could get the bowl to the floor there was a knock on the door. Ally looked through the small window in the kitchen door and saw that it was her grandmother.

"You're here bright and early." Ally smiled at her as she opened the door.

"Not that early." Charlotte glanced at her watch. "Are you ready to open the shop?"

"Just give me a minute to finish feeding the kids, and we can make some muffins for breakfast at the shop."

"Actually, I won't be able to join you today. My book club is meeting this morning to have our own little ceremony for Julia. I hope you don't mind."

"Of course not, that's fine."

"I thought I'd stop by and take Arnold for a walk before I go to the book club. Are you doing okay after last night?"

"Yes. Still a little shaken up. But more determined than ever. If Mayor Malcolm thinks he can get away with burning down someone's house to cover up his crimes he has another thing coming."

"But didn't you say the pictures didn't indicate that he had any relationship with Julia?"

"I did, but who knows what other pictures Ralph had that he didn't want seen. Whatever his reason, the message was clear."

"Still, we don't even know if he's the one that did it. At this point, we don't even know if it was arson. Ralph could have made a mistake, or it could have been faulty wiring. Personally, I'm glad that so many pictures are gone."

"I guess you're right." Ally frowned. "He did plan to manipulate some people if necessary. Although, I'm sure he has most of them backed up."

"A man like that really can't be trusted." Charlotte crossed her arms. "Anyone that would steal private moments to use them as ammunition later is not the best person in my opinion."

"Or maybe it's the only way that he knows to protect himself. However, obviously it didn't work this time."

"Maybe."

"There's one sure way we can get more information about Mayor Malcolm." Ally pulled out her phone. "It's time to tap our own resources." She selected a number and put the phone to her ear. "Hello? Mrs. Bing? It's Ally. Would you mind joining me at the shop for some taste testing?" She winked at Charlotte. Charlotte smiled her approval and hooked Arnold's leash onto his collar. As she led him out the door Ally gathered her things and followed after her.

"While you're getting the dirt, I'll do a little digging of my own. See what I can find out from my book club," Charlotte said.

"Good idea." Ally waved to her as she climbed into the car.

"Tell Mrs. Bing I say hi, and to enjoy the treats."

"I will."

On the drive to the shop Ally noticed that there was a lot of activity around one of the houses she passed. It only took her a moment to recognize Officer Frank at the corner of the property. She slowed to a stop and rolled her window down.

"What's going on, Officer Frank?"

He eyed her with impatience. "It's a police matter."

"I can see that. Is everything okay?" The

wrinkle in his forehead indicated annoyance, but Ally ignored it.

"It's part of the investigation."

"Whose house is this?" Ally tried to see past him to the front door.

"I'm going to have to ask you to move along." He pointed to the road in front of her.

"Sorry to bother you." Ally knew that a couple had moved into the house recently, but she hadn't met them yet. When she got a moment she would look into who owned it. Ally presumed that it must have something to do with Julia's murder because Officer Frank was from Freely.

When Ally arrived at the shop she prepared for her honored guest by making chocolate cupcakes. Not long after the bell rang to signal that a customer had walked inside. Ally walked out to greet her with a smile.

"Morning Mrs. Bing."

"Morning. Something smells wonderful."

Ally set a chocolate cupcake on a small plate

in front of Mrs. Bing.

"I'm so glad you were willing to come over and taste test."

"Oh sure, you can call me anytime for something like this. I adore everything you make." She took a big bite of the cupcake. As she licked the chocolate icing from her lips Ally met her eyes.

"What can you tell me about Mayor Malcolm from Freely?"

Her eyes sparkled. She finished chewing, then swallowed hard. "What do you want to know?"

"I've heard the rumors about Julia and him having an affair. I'm more interested in why he might want Julia dead. Was there any bad blood between them?"

Mrs. Bing smacked her lips together and stared at the cupcake. "Not exactly bad blood. It's more like an intense competition. You see Julia was set to run against Tim in the next election. Since she's been more present in the community and drummed up quite a bit of support there was a very good chance that she would win."

"But you don't think he would kill her over that, do you?"

"I think that some people find their identity in their position. So, if they lose that position they can suffer some severe emotional reactions. It's possible that if he felt threatened, he might have spun into a panic that made him do something rash."

Ally shook her head. "It's hard for me to believe that someone would murder for political gain."

"Please honey, people have been murdering for political gain for a very long time. However, that doesn't mean that I believe he did it. I don't know one way or another. I'm just telling you what I've observed. He's not a bad man, but he sure does have a temper, and there are plenty of people that are terrified of him."

"Yes, because of the way he runs things."

"Yes that, and his history."

"What history?" Ally looked up with interest.

"As a young adult he was involved with some of the roughest characters in Freely."

"How many rough characters could there be in Freely?"

"You don't know what it was like back then. It wasn't always such a nice, quiet place."

"I guess I don't."

"Never mind that, the important thing to remember is that it doesn't matter who the police arrest. If Mayor Malcolm is the one who did this then..."

"If I did what?" Mayor Malcolm stood in the doorway, his tense gaze fixed on Ally. Ally's heart dropped into her stomach. Not only did she not hear the bell ring over the door when he opened it, she had no idea that someone had stepped inside. One thing was certain about this man, he knew how to sneak his way into places.

"We were just talking about Julia." Ally cleared her throat.

"Julia was a beautiful woman," Mayor Malcolm said.

"Oops, look at the time, I do have to run. Bye Ally!" Mrs. Bing rushed towards the door. The moment she was gone Mayor Malcolm paused in front of the counter.

"That still doesn't answer my question. If I did what?"

Ally held his gaze. It was already clear that he had guessed what she referred to. What was the point of trying to hide it?

"The glass of champagne that you handed to Julia was laced with poison. The police know that."

"You don't think I'm aware of what the police know?" He lofted an eyebrow. "It's Ally, right?"

"Yes." Ally gripped the underside of the counter. It was the only way that she remained upright. She was so nervous that she felt as if she might faint.

"You know, the last thing that the deputy

mayor ate was one of the chocolate tarts from this very store. Is that true?"

"I don't know. I didn't see her the entire time."

"Okay, but the police did collect her plate and all that remained on it was half of the chocolate tart. Right?"

"Right." Ally continued to steady herself with the counter.

"So, who is to say that the chocolate tart wasn't laced with poison?"

"The police tested it. It came out negative."

"But what if it had come out positive? How would it make you feel, knowing that you would never do anything to hurt Julia, but that the rest of the town, including the police, believed otherwise? All based on a tiny piece of evidence that proves nothing."

Ally stared back into his hardened gaze. She didn't want to feel any sympathy for him.

"My only interest would be in justice for the woman who was murdered. If that meant that I had to be investigated, then I would happily cooperate."

He rested his hands on the counter in front of her and leaned so close that she could smell his cologne.

"I am not a very cooperative person. I take great offense to being accused of crimes that I did not commit."

"What about being accused of crimes that you did commit?" Ally's eyes widened in reaction to her own words. So did the mayor's.

"Brave young lady, hm?" He tilted his head to the side. "I wonder how long that bravery will last when you need my help with something."

"I don't often ask for help."

"I imagine you don't." He chuckled. The sound broke the tension that had built within Ally. She couldn't quite read whether she should be intimidated by the man or amused. With moments slipping by she considered what she should do next.

"Would you like a sample?" She held out a tray of chocolates.

"Can I consider this a bribe?"

"Absolutely not." She narrowed her eyes.

"All right then." He smiled slightly then plucked one of the chocolates from the tray and popped it into his mouth. "I do hope that you're not spreading too many rumors, Ally. I'd like to believe that you're wise enough to think about the consequences of a few mistruths."

"All I care about is justice, Mayor Malcolm. I'm not interested in rumors or lies."

"I guess we shall see if that's true." He met her eyes one last time, then turned to leave the shop. As he closed the door behind him Ally could finally take a full breath in. She held it for a long moment until she was sure that he wouldn't burst back through the door. Once she was, she exhaled. Her heart still pounded with the memory of his presence. Did he come in by chance and just happened to overhear their conversation? Or was he trying to send her a message directly?

Chapter Eighteen

Not long after the mayor had left the shop, another customer arrived. Ally smiled at the woman who walked inside. She had her reddish brown hair high in a ponytail and wore a cute top that featured a cat on the front.

"Oh, how adorable. I have a kitty at home."

"I have two." She smiled as she browsed the chocolates.

"Please let me know if there's anything I can help you with."

"Actually, I was wondering if you do gift baskets?"

"Absolutely." Ally pulled out a small brochure that featured the shop's most popular gift baskets. "I can always make one custom to your choices as well."

"Oh, how wonderful. I think I'd like to have this one. It's a present for my brother and sister-in-law to thank them for helping us move house."

She tapped the picture. "I'm sure they will adore all of these chocolates."

"Great. I can have that ready for you in about an hour."

"Really, so fast? Wonderful!" She smiled. "I guess I'll be back to pick it up then."

"If you'd like we offer free delivery to the local area with all of our gift baskets. I'll be closing up just about that time so if you live nearby and it's easier for you I can just run it over to you."

"That would be perfect." She pulled out her phone. "Let me give you the address." Her eyes glazed as she looked at her phone. "Huh. Something strange is going on at the house. Anyway, here's the address." She jotted it down on the slip of paper Ally offered her. "Either I or my husband Kevin will be there."

"Great. I'll throw in a few extra chocolate samples so they can have a bigger choice."

"Wow, that's so kind of you."

Once the sale was settled Ally followed her to

the door. She noticed the woman looked at her phone again and her expression grew even more troubled.

"Is everything okay?"

"Yes. There's just some kind of misunderstanding. It's fine I'm sure. Thank you again for delivering the basket."

"It's my pleasure."

Ally closed the door behind her after she had stepped out. She set about preparing the basket of chocolates and muffins for delivery. By the time she was done it was past closing time. It had been quite a busy day. No customers mentioned a word about the deputy mayor's death or who might have been involved. She was more than a little discouraged by the lack of new leads. Once more she considered whether it might make sense to break into the mayor's home. She had to get some kind of solid evidence before it was too late.

After locking up Ally glanced at her watch. It was close to two hours since the basket was ordered and she hoped that the customer wouldn't mind too much that she was late. She hurried out to her car and took a deep breath as she once more talked herself out of breaking into the mayor's home. She knew that it would only put her more at risk. But without gathering much information, and her encounter with him that day, she felt even more anxious to get to the truth.

Ally knew the street that the delivery was going to so she started her car and took off down the road. It wasn't long before she arrived at the house. It wasn't until she looked at it that she realized that it was the same house she'd seen the police at earlier in the day. She recalled the troubled look on the woman's face as she received messages on her phone. Perhaps they were about the police investigation? Ally was uneasy, but she needed to deliver the package. The police were gone, so they obviously hadn't found anything. She grabbed the basket from the backseat and headed up the front walkway. When she reached the front door she could hear voices on the other side.

"I don't understand why the police were here, Kevin? Why did all of the neighbors see our house being searched by the police? We have just moved here and they are going to think we are criminals."

"If you would just calm down. You're overreacting."

"Am I?"

Ally decided to knock on the door before she was caught eavesdropping. She knocked and then braced herself.

"Someone's at the door."

"I don't care who's at the door. You get it, my hands are full," the woman said.

Ally stepped back from the door. Now she was sure that this was the same house where she'd seen the police earlier in the day. With this on her mind she wondered what kind of volatile situation she might be walking into.

"Answer the door!" The man demanded.

Ally cringed. The door jerked open. The sweet woman she'd seen earlier in the day was red-faced when she looked at Ally. "What?"

"I'm delivering your gift basket," Ally stumbled out the words.

"Oh yes, right. I'm sorry." She sighed. "Could you bring it inside for me? My hands are full of flour."

Ally noticed that the woman held a dish towel in her hand and her hands really were covered in flour. She wondered if it was a good idea to go inside. The two could be up to something criminal. Her curiosity won however and she nodded.

"Absolutely, I can do that. Just show me where you want it."

"I guess the kitchen table would be the safest place right now. I'm trying a new recipe and let's just say it got a little out of control." Ally noticed that there was no sign of the male whose voice that she'd heard through the door. The woman washed and dried her hands.

"I understand. That happens to me

sometimes." Ally set the gift basket down on the table. As she did she noticed a set of glasses lined up on a shelf just above the counter. When she saw them her heart jumped. They had a diamond pattern. There were water, wine and champagne glasses all neatly lined up. They were the same as the glasses that Julia was poisoned from. The same as the glass she'd found in the mayor's office. How could that be? Was it just a coincidence? As she stared at the glasses, the woman walked towards her.

"Uh, is something wrong? Am I supposed to tip you or something?" The woman wrapped an arm around her body and grabbed her elbow with the other hand. Ally was familiar with the stance. She seemed nervous of something.

"I was just wondering where you got those glasses from?"

"Those?" She rolled her eyes. "Everyone wants to know about those glasses today. They were a gift from the mayor of Freely."

"Do you know the mayor?"

"No. They weren't a gift to me. They were a gift to my brother. My sister-in-law didn't want them, so she gave them to me."

"That's a pretty special gift."

"Not really, everyone who signed a contract to provide services to Freely last year got them as gifts from Mayor Malcolm."

"That's a nice gesture." Ally smiled.

"I guess." She shrugged as she looked at them. Ally noticed that there were only five champagne flutes, but six of the other glasses. She looked around for the missing glass in the sink, but there were no dirty dishes.

"Looks like one is missing."

"Yes, it went missing in the move."

"I hope you enjoy the basket."

"Thank you. I'm sure that Scott and Maddie will." Ally's eyes widened at the mention of the names.

As she walked out of the house she realized that the woman's brother must be Scott Brally.

She left the house in a daze. If the police were investigating Scott's relatives then they had to have good reason. She suddenly had an idea. What if the murderer hadn't put the glass on the table, but had given it to a staff member at the country club to put on the table? She decided to take a spin by the country club and have a conversation with some of the employees there.

Chapter Nineteen

Ally parked close to the side entrance of the country club. It was the same door she'd entered with a box full of tarts on the fateful night of Julia's death. It felt strange to walk back towards it. However, she knew that the door might lead to the answers that she needed in order to find Julia's murderer. She pushed the door open and found herself immediately immersed in a flood of staff members.

"Excuse me." A man brushed past her and joined the rest of the crowd as they headed down a long hallway.

Ally grabbed the arm of Elisa, the woman who was in charge of catering on the night of the cocktail party.

"Ally."

"Hi Elisa." Ally smiled. "What's happening? Where is everyone going?"

"Oh, there's a special training session. After

what happened with the deputy mayor heads are going to roll."

"What do you mean?" Ally fell into step beside her.

"Well, obviously the mayor had a glass that he shouldn't have had. We don't allow people to bring in outside dishware."

"Why not?"

"Just for this reason. We can't guarantee its safety or cleanliness. The police think that what most likely happened is that the glass had poison in it so that when champagne was added the champagne would become poisoned. It was brought in from outside."

"I see. So, who do you think is going to get in trouble for this?"

"Merla, no doubt. She is the one that let the glass in."

"She did?"

"Yes, she bowed to the pressure of the mayor's assistant and gave in to allowing him to use his usual champagne glass for the toast. She said it was his lucky one. It shouldn't have been a big deal, but considering what happened." She sighed. "Poor girl doesn't even know what's coming."

"Do you think I could speak to her? Where is she?"

"There." She pointed off to the side near the double doors that all of the other staff members flooded through. A young woman leaned against a wall and plucked at her phone. Ally gritted her teeth. She looked very young, too young perhaps to even understand the enormity of what she was involved in. Unless of course money exchanging hands was the reason she accepted the glass. Either way, she wanted to speak to her.

Ally took a deep breath and walked up to her. "Hi there." She smiled at her. The girl looked up from her phone with a quirked eyebrow.

"Hi?"

"My name is Ally. Are you Merla?"

She narrowed her eyes. "Don't I know you from somewhere?"

"I run the chocolate shop in Blue River."

"Oh yes!" She smiled. "One of my favorite places. That candy is to die for." She winced. "Maybe that's not the right way to put it."

"It's okay. Don't worry. I'm not here to cause you any trouble."

"You're the only one." She pursed her lips and looked down at her phone again. "I know I'm getting fired today, the only thing I'm not sure about is whether I'm getting arrested."

"Arrested? For what?"

"Haven't you heard?" She looked back up at Ally. "I'm the one who killed Julia Turnamas."

"Sh!" Ally looked around fast, then tugged her away from the door. "You should certainly not be making statements like that."

"I don't mean that I really killed her, but I provided the murder weapon. That's what the detective told me."

"Listen, it's a detective's job to intimidate you, to put you on edge, that's the easiest way to get information out of you. Try not to be too worried."

"How can I not be? I made a mistake that cost someone their life."

"Merla, how old are you?"

"I just turned eighteen. This is my first real job and I stuffed it up." She frowned.

"Listen, if it wasn't you, it would have been someone else. Okay? It's not your fault that she's dead."

"You don't think so?" She looked back down at her phone again. Ally caught sight of a few tears glimmering in her eyes.

"I don't think so. In fact, I know it's not. But you might just be the only person that can help figure out who did do this."

"How can I do that?"

"Anything you can remember about the person who gave you the glass will make a difference."

"That's the thing, I can't remember. It was so busy, and I was so nervous. I was sure I would drop something or spill something on someone. All I could think about was getting through the night. When the woman stopped me to give me the glass, I had no idea what to do. Since she said she was the mayor's assistant, I thought it was okay to take the glass from her."

"Of course you did. Why wouldn't it be? But what can you tell me about the woman?"

"Like I said, she was the mayor's assistant."

"I know what she told you, but what did she look like? Was she old or young? Tall or short? Did it look like she could be wearing a disguise?"

"She was wearing a hat, it covered most of her hair. I'm not sure if you would really call that a disguise. She was tall, and really young."

"You're calling someone else young?"

"I mean she probably wasn't much older than me. I remember because I felt a little bad, here I am at my first job, and she's in a position as important as the mayor's assistant." She shrugged. "But then she popped her gum, and I wasn't as impressed."

"Young and chewing gum? Blonde?"

"I think so. She had her hair under a hat, but I could see a few strands. I mean, I can't be absolutely sure."

"She never gave her name?"

"No, just her title. I should have asked, I know. I should have done a lot of things that I didn't." Her cheeks flushed. "Looking back on it now I can't believe I was that stupid."

"You weren't stupid, Merla. You did what you thought was the right thing to do. It was a busy night with a lot of important people. To be honest with you if we were hosting an event at the chocolate shop I might have done the same thing. I can't promise you that there won't be any consequences for what happened, but I can tell you that you will get through this. It's a bump in the road. Don't let it color the rest of your life. Okay?"

"I'll try." She looked towards the door as the last staff member walked through it. "But I'm not sure that I can get past this."

Ally rested her hand on her shoulder and gave it a light squeeze. "Maybe you can, if we find the person who did this. If my hunch is right, I think you just helped a lot."

"I hope so." She shoved her phone in her pocket. "I have to go face the firing squad now. Thanks for your support. I really needed it."

"No problem, if you ever need anything, you know where to find me." Ally smiled at her.

"Thanks." She nodded and headed through the door. Ally had to give her credit for the fact that she even went, knowing what she might face. At eighteen she likely would have run off somewhere to hide until the storm blew over. Or maybe she wouldn't have. Luckily, she didn't have to face that choice at such a young age. Now she had a choice to make. She could run off and hide, and wait for the police to come to the same conclusion she had, or she could pursue it.

Without question she knew what her choice was. On her way back out to the car she placed a phone call.

"This is Kristy, how may I help you?" She popped her gum. Ally narrowed her eyes.

"Sorry, wrong number." Ally hung up the phone. Her heart pounded. She still had no real evidence, but she had a very good idea of what had happened, and she was determined to follow it through. It was time to make the visit she had been putting off. Hopefully by the end of the night, a murderer would be in jail.

Chapter Twenty

Ally stopped by Freely Lakes and knocked on her grandmother's door.

"Ally?" She hugged her. "What are you doing here?"

"I was hoping you'd feed Arnold and Peaches for me, and maybe take Arnold for a walk. I have to check on something."

"What?"

"Not the mayor, don't worry. I don't even think he's the killer anymore."

"Wait, what are you thinking?" Charlotte's eyes widened.

"Well, everything is pointing back towards Scott Brally."

"What would his motivation be?"

"There was a good chance that he was going to lose the contract he had for the waste at Freely. Maybe that loss was motivation enough to try to get rid of not only the deputy mayor, but also the mayor."

"Or maybe he wasn't even targeting Julia." Charlotte frowned. "Maybe he was after Mayor Malcolm the whole time and it was just an unfortunate coincidence that he handed her his glass of champagne."

"Either way I think that there's good reason to be concerned about him." Ally narrowed her eyes.

"So, what is your plan?"

"If he is the one that poisoned the champagne glass, then maybe I can find something to incriminate him. Maybe he has a receipt for the purchase of some kind of poison, or maybe he wrote out his plan. The only way to find that out is to go to his house."

"You mean try and break into his house?" Charlotte shook her head.

"I'm not going to break in. I'm just going to pay him a visit. Maybe he'll invite me in or maybe he won't."

"Ally, if you really believe that he is the murderer then you need to do everything in your power to avoid being alone with him."

"I know that you're right about that. All I want to do is take a look around his house and see if anything jumps out at me."

"Then I'm going to come with you."

"I don't think that's a good idea, Mee-Maw. I need you to be available in case I need back- up. Can you do that?"

"You know I can. Although, I'd rather be there with you."

"Don't worry I'll keep you updated I promise." Ally hugged her and then glanced at her watch. "It's still early enough for me to get over to his place and wait for him to get home from work."

"Please be careful."

"I will be." Ally looked into her eyes. "Hopefully we can put an end to all of this."

"I hope so."

Charlotte looked as if she might stop her as she walked away, but Ally didn't wait to find out. She'd have the best chance of getting some information out of him if she surprised him. Maybe he would slip up if he wasn't forewarned.

**

Ally found a spot a few houses down. Then she got out of the car and scoped out a place to hide out. A tall group of bushes seemed like the perfect place. She crouched down behind the bushes and peered through the branches. If there was anything to see by the front door she had a good view, but other than that she couldn't see anything.

As she waited for Scott to return from work she thought through her options. So far speaking to him directly hadn't worked. Maybe if she could record him talking to someone else he might incriminate himself. However, what if he didn't talk? If she could get some evidence that he had the glass in his possession at some point that would point to him as the killer. But since she presumed that the rest of the glasses were at his sister's house, she had no idea how she could make that happen. The only real possibility was to get inside and see if she could find evidence of poison in the house.

Since the driveway was empty and she assumed there was still at least an hour before he would get home, Ally decided that she should see if she could see into the house through a window or if there were any open doors or windows. She crept along the side of the house. She couldn't see anything incriminating through the windows and she found that every door and window was locked. When she peered through the kitchen window she was startled to see that a woman sat at the kitchen table. Ally ducked out of the way before she could be spotted. His wife was home? She cringed at what might have happened if she'd succeeded at breaking in. How could she have explained herself to his wife? Once she got over her initial shock she realized that this was a good opportunity. She walked back to the front of the house and rang the bell. As she formed excuses for being at the door she came up with one that she thought would be foolproof. The woman came to the door and raised an eyebrow when she saw Ally. Ally recognized her straight away as the woman that was with Scott at the cocktail party, she just hoped that she didn't recognize Ally.

"Can I help you?"

"I'm so sorry to bother you. My car broke down, and my cell phone is dead. I'm not sure which way to go for a gas station. Is it possible to borrow your phone?" She began to cough.

"Oh, you poor thing. There isn't a gas station or shop for miles. Let me get the phone for you." She started to turn away. Ally coughed even louder. "Are you okay?" She turned back.

"I'm sorry, I just have this scratch in my throat." Ally coughed again. "I think I have some cough drops in the car."

"Why don't you just come in? I'll get you something to drink."

"Are you sure it's not too much bother?"

"It's fine." She smiled as she studied her. "There's something familiar about you. Are you sure I haven't met you before?"

"No, I don't think so." Ally braced herself. Would the woman recognize her from the cocktail party? Would the woman remember her voice from their phone conversation?

"Okay. Here's the phone, just sit down and I'll get you a glass of water."

"Thanks so much." Ally took the phone and followed her into the kitchen. Right away she began to look around for any matching glasses. She also skimmed the area for any out of place bottles or vials. From what the officer had told her grandmother she knew that the poison was a clear liquid as it was undetected in an empty glass, but she didn't know much more about it. As she dialed her grandmother's number, her cell phone began to ring in her pocket. Her heart lurched as she wondered how she was stupid enough to leave it on.

"I thought you said your phone was dead?" Maddie turned to face her with a glass in her hand.

"Oh, I'm sorry I thought it was. It must have had enough juice in it for one last call."

"Huh. Yeah, phones can be funny that way." She turned to the refrigerator and pulled out a bottle of water. Ally noticed that the bottle was sealed. She set the glass down on the counter in front of her. Ally couldn't see it anymore.

"Hello?"

"Mee-Maw, it's me. The car broke down, and my phone isn't working."

"It is working, I just called you. What do you mean your car broke down?"

"This nice woman let me use her phone to call for help. Is there any way you can come to pick me up?"

"Ally, what's going on? Are you in trouble?"

Ally rattled off the address. "Thanks Mee-Maw. You know how the car is always acting up, you never can tell when it's going to do something unexpected."

"Ally, you went inside? Are you safe? I'll be there as fast as I can."

"Yes, I'm all right, no car accident, it was just a breakdown. As soon as you can get here would be great. Thanks." Ally hung up the phone. Maddie turned around to face her and carried a glass of water over to the table.

"Is someone coming?"

"Yes, I'll just wait outside for her." Ally started to stand up.

"Nonsense. Sit down and rest a little. Drink your water." She locked eyes with Ally. Something about the way she looked at her made Ally's heart drop.

"Thanks." Ally grasped the glass. She noticed that the outside seemed a little slippery, as if oil had spilled on it. Her heart began to race. What if Maddie was in on it? What if she suspected Ally and poisoned the water? By giving her grandmother the address was she leading her straight towards danger? She had told her where she was for the plan to work because she needed someone to come pick her up, but had she just made a huge mistake and put her grandmother at risk.

"Aren't you going to drink it? You were practically choking to death earlier."

"Oh, yes of course I will, in just a minute." Ally cleared her throat.

"You know, you told me we don't know each other. But I think we do."

"Oh?" Ally studied her. "Maybe you've been to the chocolate shop in Blue River? I'm the manager there."

"Is that so?" She tilted her head to the side. "Yes, I remember you now. Weren't you serving tarts at the dinner when Deputy Mayor Julia Turnamas died? My husband said he was speaking to you."

"Yes, I was. I'm not sure if I know your

husband though."

"Oh, I'm sure that you do." She sat down across from Ally and pushed the glass of water towards her. "Drink up. Unless there's some reason you don't want to?" Maddie smirked. The look in her eyes was as cold as steel. Could Maddie be the murderer? All of a sudden Maddie's face relaxed and her eyes became welcoming. Ally wandered if she was just being paranoid.

Ally stared at the glass of water. She faced a difficult decision. If she refused to drink the water then Maddie would know that she suspected her. If she did drink the water she risked being poisoned herself. She preferred to think that Maddie wouldn't do that, but she couldn't know for sure.

"I'm sorry, I like my water to be room temperature before I drink. The cold just hits my teeth wrong." She sighed and touched her jaw. "I've been meaning to get to the dentist, but you know how that is. Who wants to voluntarily go somewhere that they're going to put a drill into your mouth?"

"Good question." Maddie laughed. "So how do you enjoy running the chocolate shop?"

"It's great. I get to be surrounded by good smells, good food and good people."

"I guess you get to know a lot of the people around town by working there."

"Yes, I do."

"So, what are you doing all the way out here?" She raised an eyebrow. "It's a long drive."

"I know. Actually I am looking into buying a house out here. I thought I had the address right, but I think I had it wrong, because I got lost."

"And you just happened to end up here?" Maddie smiled. "Lucky girl."

"Yes, that seems to be the case." Ally smiled.

"Odd that you'd want to buy a house all the way out here, when you work in Blue River." She tapped a finger lightly on the table top.

"Oh, you know, you have to go where you can

afford."

"You must be joking." She laughed. "The house prices around here are through the roof compared to Blue River. You're single, aren't you? I don't see a ring. I'm sure you could pick up a little house in Blue River for a real steal."

"Oh, you may be right." Ally laughed to cover her discomfort. "Maybe I wasn't thinking clearly. Like I said, I never found the house, I got lost."

"Yes, you mentioned getting lost, and ending up here, Ally."

She lifted her eyes to meet Maddie's. Her stomach flipped. There was no question that the woman knew that her story was a lie.

"I should go outside, my grandmother is probably waiting for me."

"No, please, stay. Drink your water." Maddie pushed it closer to her.

"I'm not really thirsty anymore."

Maddie smirked. "I don't care."

"Excuse me?"

"You have two options. You can drink the water, or I can pour it down your throat. I promise you, you're not going to enjoy it if I do that."

"What are you talking about?"

"I know exactly who you are. You're the one that called my husband's office to ask about an appointment. You're the one that alerted the police that he'd made some less than flattering comments about Julia, and caused him so much stress. He's still upset about that, and worried that people in the community will think that he was somehow involved in her murder. That's a terrible thing to put such a good man through."

"So, he didn't know?" Ally's eyes widened. "You killed Julia alone?"

"Ally, do you know what it's like to see a man work hours, upon hours? He worked so hard that he had to go on medications for his stress. Then finally, he got a contract with Freely, it was the break we were waiting for. We were able to afford this house, and we settled in to have a chance to finally stop struggling so much and enjoy our lives. Then out of the blue, all of that is threatened. It's all going to be taken away. It doesn't matter how hard we worked, all that matters is that his business doesn't have the right zip code. How is that fair?"

Ally stared across the table at her. "It's not."

"I know. My poor husband wept over it. You've seen him. Does he look like a man who cries easily?"

"No." Ally lowered her eyes as her heart pounded harder. "But, you don't need to take things any further than that. I know you did what you did out of love for your husband. No one is going to hold that against you."

"Liar." She laughed. "How stupid do you think I am? I'll be going to jail, for life. But not today I won't. You should have left my husband alone. You should have let the mayor take the rap. It's not like he's a great guy to begin with. Instead, you got yourself involved. So, now you have to go. Drink the water." She gestured to the glass. "Now!" Her shout made Ally jump. She was not about to drink the water. The question was, how could she get away with not drinking it? She reached for the glass. As soon as her hands touched the outside she remembered how slick and oily it had felt. With wide, fear filled eyes she picked up the glass and pretended that she was going to drink it. Instead she let the glass slip out of her hand. It crashed to the floor and shattered.

"Oh, you think you get out of it that easily?" Maddie jumped up and grabbed Ally by her hair. She slammed her head down into the top of the table before Ally could even think about defending herself. The sharp pain that flooded her made her head spin. She tried to stand up, but that only made her more dizzy. As the room flipped upside down she crashed into the floor.

"There. You had to choose the hard way." She heard the clap of the woman's palms. Her head still screamed in pain. She kept her eyes closed and hoped that Maddie would think she was knocked out. If she did, she might be able to buy herself some time. She remained still on the floor and kept her breath shallow. Now, she wished with all of her heart that she hadn't come to the house, that she hadn't called her grandmother. What was it that made her think she was invincible? This was proof enough that she was not. At any moment everything could come to an end, and it was all because she was too stubborn to be cautious. Sometime later a sharp knock jolted her from her thoughts. At first she thought the knocking sound was the pounding of her head. Then she began to piece together that the sound came from a distance. She heard footsteps as Maddie walked away. Then she heard voices.

"May I help you?"

"Yes, I'm looking for my granddaughter, Ally? She called me and told me she would be here."

Ally's heart pounded harder than her head. She had lead her grandmother into danger. Would her grandmother be Maddie's next victim?

"Oh, I'm sorry, she already left. I believe she had someone else pick her up. All I know is she got a phone call and headed out the door."

"A phone call from who?"

"She didn't say. Nice girl though."

"Maybe I should give her a call."

"Sure."

Ally knew that she'd turned her phone off. She willed her hand to go to her cell phone and turn it back on. If her grandmother heard the ring she would know that she was still in the house. Even though Ally could think it, she couldn't get her body to act. The buzzing in her mind grew even louder. She was aware that blood trickled from where her head had hit the table. Darkness closed in from all sides, indicating she might not be conscious long.

"Her phone is not picking up."

"She did say it was dead."

"I guess I'll just have to go look for her car."

"Good idea. Like I said, she probably got picked up by someone else."

"Right."

Ally heard the door close. In the back of her mind she was aware that her grandmother knew better, but that didn't stop the panic within her. Would anyone figure it out in time to save her? Ally heard footsteps as the woman walked back towards the kitchen. Each step felt like a countdown to her final breath.

Chapter Twenty-One

Charlotte walked away from the house with an uneasy sensation in the pit of her stomach. Down the block she could see Ally's car parked along the road. Maybe Luke picked her up. But surely Luke would have texted her and let her know. She sent a quick text to him just to be sure.

Did you pick up Ally?

A few seconds later she received a reply.

No, everything okay?

Charlotte didn't bother to respond. She turned back towards the house and wondered what might be happening. Was the wife involved? Ally could be in grave danger and she had no idea how to protect her. Her phone buzzed with a few more texts. She saw that they were from Luke, but she didn't bother to read them. Instead she made her way around the side of the house. She tried to see in the windows, but she couldn't see anything of interest. She pressed her ear close to one. She

243

didn't hear any voices. Her stomach churned with fear. Without a second thought she dialed the number for Officer Frank. She wasn't going to risk the possibility that Ally was somewhere inside the house in need of help. As she dialed she walked away from the house. If she was spotted that might force the killer's hand.

***

As Ally continued to play dead she began to think of life in terms of minutes rather than years. The more she tried to focus on how she could escape, the more her head hurt. She forced her eyes open just as Maddie returned to the kitchen.

"Let me go, I didn't do anything to you."

"That's not an option I'm afraid. I don't think you understand just how important it is to me that my husband is happy. I don't think he would be too happy about his wife going to prison. Do you?"

"I doubt he'd be too happy that you're a murderer."

"Which is something that he will never find

out." She pulled her hair back into a ponytail. "Now let's get this over with as I'm sure I'll have a lot of cleaning up to do."

Ally's heart lurched. She was about to be murdered by a woman who was only concerned with the cleanliness of her kitchen. There was no way that she could reason with her. But could she stall her?

"Why did you kill her? How did you know that the mayor would give her his glass of champagne?"

"I didn't. The mayor was the target." She shrugged. "But either way it worked. Both signatures are needed to change the contract. Now, there's only one."

"What about Ted Housers? He could sign with the mayor."

"He could, but he won't. Ted's not a problem. You see, if Mayor Malcolm was dead, then Julia would take his place, and Ted would take her place. Ted will never sign for local contractors, because he knows that I know about his relationship with Julia. I would out her for the cheater that she is."

"But Julia is dead now. What does it matter?"

"It matters because Ted is married, too. You'd be surprised what lengths people will go to, just to keep their dirty little secrets. Disgusting." She scrunched up her nose. "It's not as if Julia is a great loss."

Ally swallowed back angry words and tried to focus on continuing to stall the woman.

"How did you get Kristy to drop off the champagne glass?"

"That was easy. She had no idea it was poisoned and then when she realized what was happening I just offered her some more money."

"Did you burn down Ralph's house?" Ally asked as the thought suddenly occurred to her.

"No." She giggled. "That was Ted. Ralph was blackmailing him about his relationship with Julia." Ally thought about it all being a waste as the truth about Julia and Ted had now been revealed.

"Killing me isn't going to solve anything. I'm not the only one that knows what you did."

"Nice try." She laughed. "You didn't even know, at least not for sure. No one else knows. Your grandmother smiled at me like I was the sweetest person she'd ever met. Who else would you tell?"

"The police. I told the police. They know that you gave Kristy the glass to take to the party for the mayor. When I go missing, they're going to come after you."

"You have no proof, the police probably laughed in your face. And trust me honey, it's going to be some time before they can find your body."

"Don't do this, don't do this." Ally gave up her pride and began to beg. It flashed through her mind that her grandmother would be left alone. That Peaches would never understand why she didn't come home. As she pleaded with Maddie for her life, she promised inwardly that she would never take such a great risk again, if only somehow she was able to get out of the situation.

"Please stop your blubbering. Really, it's embarrassing." She rolled her eyes and lunged towards Ally. "I told you to drink the water, I'll get another glass of poisoned water so you can have one last chance to drink the poison. Otherwise I'll have to use other methods."

Ally swallowed hard. Maybe the poison would be the better choice. She opened her mouth to speak, but before she could the back door burst open. Luke charged into the kitchen with his gun drawn. "Back away from her! Now!"

Ally's eyes widened as Maddie jumped and stumbled back. She raised her hands in the air.

"This woman's crazy. She accused me of murder and then she tried to attack me. She's crazy!"

"Ally, get back." Luke shot her a stern look then returned his gaze to Maddie. "Turn around and put your hands on your head."

"Please, you have it all wrong. This is my house, she conned her way inside and then tried to kill me!"

"Save it." Luke moved closer to her. Outside the house sirens shrieked through the air. Ally blinked back tears of relief. She managed to pull herself up into a sitting position. With one hand pressed to the cut on her head she watched in a daze as Luke handcuffed Maddie.

"Does she have a weapon, Ally?"

Ally pointed to the broken glass on the floor. "Poison. She tried to poison me."

"Did you drink any of it?" Luke's eyes filled with fear.

"Not a drop." Ally rested her head back against the wall and sighed. "Not a drop."

He scooped her up in his arms and carried her out of the house. Ally didn't protest, or point out that she could probably walk just fine on her own. Instead she rested her head against his chest and murmured gratitude for the fact that he was there.

Outside of the house a paramedic rushed up to Ally and escorted her to the back of an ambulance. Charlotte joined her just as the paramedic applied a bandage to the cut on her head.

"Are you okay, Ally?" She touched her cheek. "Did she do that to you?"

"I'm okay. It's just a cut."

"It's a bit more than a cut." The paramedic frowned. "We're going to have to take you to the hospital. They can watch you overnight for a concussion."

"No please, I don't want to go to the hospital." Ally pulled away from the paramedic. "I just want to go home."

"With a blow to your head like that, it's best if you're observed. Do you live alone?"

"I'll stay with her." Charlotte wrapped her hand around Ally's. "I'll watch her." She smiled a little. "Remember that time you thought you could do a back flip with your bike, Ally? I sat up

250

all night then, watching for the signs of a concussion."

"Yes." Ally laughed a little. "You taught me how to play rummy."

"Yes." Charlotte squeezed her hand as tears filled her eyes. "I'm so glad that you're okay."

"I am, Mee-Maw, thanks to Luke. How did he even know where I was?"

Charlotte helped her out of the back of the ambulance. "Uh well, that might be my doing."

"What do you mean?" Ally raised an eyebrow.

"I was worried about you. After I told Luke about you breaking into the mayor's office he asked me to text him all of the information we found out about the case. He had just come back because his training was finished, but he didn't tell me he was back yet."

Luke walked across the front lawn of the property towards them both. Ally could see the concern in the furrow of his brow.

"I'm okay." She smiled at him. "Since you

came to my rescue."

"You scared me, Ally. When I saw you on the floor, and the blood..." His voice cut off. Ally reached up and stroked his cheek.

"I'm okay, Luke. I promise."

He nodded and searched her eyes. "Why would you put yourself in such a dangerous position?"

"I didn't know that I had. I was just going to talk to her husband, who I thought was the killer, but when I saw her there I thought I would talk to her instead to see if she knew anything. I had to make up a story and I thought if I could get inside and find the poison or some other evidence then the case would be broken. To be honest, I had no idea that she was the killer. Her husband didn't know anything about it. How did you know to come here?"

"When your grandmother told me that you were determined to speak to him, I did some looking into him and Maddie. I found nothing solid on him, but Maddie has had several people die under unusual circumstances in her life. A rival on the cheer leading squad when she was a teenager, a college professor that threatened to fail her, and even a waitress that she got into a squabble with over supposedly flirting with her husband. All three people died of undetermined causes. I thought that could mean poison, so I decided that I needed to get back here before you did something to put yourself at risk. I guess my hunch was right."

"I'm so lucky." Ally shook her head. "She is a sick woman."

"Very." He sighed and shook his head. "All that matters is that you are safe." He touched the bandage lightly. "And not too hurt."

"Just a little. It'll be better by morning, after a few good games of rummy."

"Rummy? I've never learned to play. Can I join?" He smiled at Ally and Charlotte.

"Absolutely." Ally smiled. "Is that okay with you, Mee-Maw?"

"Oh trust me, Ally, I think it's very clear that you need more than one set of watchful eyes looking out for you." She elbowed Luke and smiled. "I could use the help."

"Hey!" Ally laughed. "I'm not that bad."

Luke and Charlotte exchanged a look and laughed as well.

"I feel like something sweet. I'll pick up some chocolates from the shop on the way home," Charlotte said.

"Chocolate, rummy and good company. It doesn't get better than that!" Ally smiled.

As Ally followed Luke over to the detective assigned to the case she felt a sense of peace. Julia had her justice, and Maddie would never be able to hurt anyone again.

The End

Chocolate Ganache Tart Recipe

Ingredients:

Pastry:

3 cups all-purpose flour

2/3 cup confectioners' sugar

2 tablespoons cocoa powder

7 ounces unsalted butter

1 large egg

Ganache:

4 ounces semisweet chocolate

4 ounces bittersweet chocolate

2 ounces unsalted butter

1 cup heavy cream

1/4 teaspoon salt

Decoration:

1 cup fresh raspberries

Preparation:

This recipe will make 8 mini tarts. You will need 4 inch tart pans with removable bottoms.

For the pastry sift the flour, confectioners' sugar and cocoa powder into a large bowl.

Add the cubed, cold butter to the bowl with the flour mixture. Rub the flour mixture and butter together using your fingertips until the butter is incorporated and the mixture is crumbly. Don't overwork the mixture.

Gently mix in the egg and shape the mixture into a disk.

Wrap the pastry in plastic wrap and put in the fridge for about thirty minutes.

When the pastry is cold preheat the oven to 350 degrees Fahrenheit.

Take the cooled pastry out of the fridge. Divide into 8 portions and using a floured rolling pin roll into a circular shape until about 1/4 of an inch thick. Press into tart pans and remove excess mixture from the sides.

Prick the bottom of the pastry twice with a fork and then place in the fridge for five minutes. Remove from the fridge and line the tarts with parchment paper and baking beads. Place in the oven on the middle rack and bake for about 10 minutes. Remove the parchment paper and beads and bake the shell for another 5 minutes. Or until the shell is crispy and cooked through. Once cooked put aside to cool.

While the tarts are cooking you can start on the ganache filling. To make the ganache chop the chocolate and butter into small pieces and put in a large bowl. Put it aside.

Heat the cream until it is just simmering.

Pour the cream over the chocolate and butter and leave for 2-3 minutes. Then gently stir the mixture until the butter and chocolate have melted. Mix in the salt.

Put the mixture aside to cool to room temperature.

Once the ganache and tart shells are at room temperature spoon the mixture into the shells.

Place in the fridge for at least 2 hours until the ganache sets. Remove from the fridge at least an hour before serving.

Decorate with fresh raspberries.

Enjoy!

More Cozy Mysteries by Cindy Bell

Chocolate Centered Cozy Mysteries

The Sweet Smell of Murder

A Deadly Delicious Delivery

A Bitter Sweet Murder

Sage Gardens Cozy Mysteries

Birthdays Can Be Deadly

Money Can Be Deadly

Trust Can Be Deadly

Ties Can Be Deadly

Rocks Can Be Deadly

Jewelry Can Be Deadly

Numbers Can Be Deadly

Dune House Cozy Mysteries

Seaside Secrets

Boats and Bad Guys

Treasured History

Hidden Hideaways

Dodgy Dealings

Suspects and Surprises

Wendy the Wedding Planner Cozy Mysteries

Matrimony, Money and Murder

Chefs, Ceremonies and Crimes

Knives and Nuptials

Mice, Marriage and Murder

Heavenly Highland Inn Cozy Mysteries

Murdering the Roses

Dead in the Daisies

Killing the Carnations

Drowning the Daffodils

Suffocating the Sunflowers

Books, Bullets and Blooms

A Deadly serious Gardening Contest

A Bridal Bouquet and a Body

Bekki the Beautician Cozy Mysteries

Hairspray and Homicide

A Dyed Blonde and a Dead Body

Mascara and Murder

Pageant and Poison

Conditioner and a Corpse

Mistletoe, Makeup and Murder

Hairpin, Hair Dryer and Homicide

Blush, a Bride and a Body

Shampoo and a Stiff

Cosmetics, a Cruise and a Killer

Lipstick, a Long Iron and Lifeless

Camping, Concealer and Criminals

Treated and Dyed